BLUE HORIZONS

The itinerary of the magnificent ocean liner *ss Regina* read New York, Florida, the West Indies, South America. A trip of a lifetime for the passengers but not for personnel – especially in the Sick Bay. To recover from a broken engagement, Nurse Owen turned for help to her wealthy uncle, chairman of the shipping line, who quickly arranged the job on the *Regina*. Full of romantic ideas about life at sea, her first shock came when she met Dr. Mike Halliday. One look was sufficient for open warfare to be declared in the Sick Bay. And with her ex-fiancé, Colin Butler, on board, shipboard life was far from smooth-sailing for the pretty niece of the chairman . . .

BLUE HORIZONS

JESSICA BLAKE

MILLS & BOON LIMITED
London . Sydney . Toronto

First published in Great Britain 1977 by Mills & Boon
Limited, 17–19 Foley Street, London W1A 1DR.

ISBN 0 263 72549 9

Set in 10 on 12pt Baskerville

Made and Printed in Great Britain by
C. Nicholls & Company Ltd
The Philips Park Press, Manchester

CHAPTER ONE

WHEN Colin broke off their engagement, Lesley refused to believe it. He wouldn't do a thing like that, hurting her as well as himself.

"But it's your happiness I'm thinking of, darling, not mine. I am standing in the way of a better marriage for you, and now your father is dead it's even more true. You're used to luxury. You've always had it."

"It has gone now."

"All the more reason why you shouldn't remain tied to me."

"But your job has prospects, and you must admit you live at a pretty good pace."

"Only because the company expects it. I'm a sort of P.R. man really, going on these cruise ships as a courier for Baynards Travel Agency, arranging trips ashore for passengers who have booked through them and increasing their business by getting more clients. My expense account is for wooing the right people and subtly persuading them to book future holidays through us. It benefits the Owen Shipping Line as well as Baynards, a fact your uncle should appreciate. He will know well enough that my expense account isn't for living on."

"I can work."

"At what? My sweet, you've never had to and what on earth could you do?"

"Nursing, of course. I trained."

"But never took it up."

"Because I had to nurse Father. He would have no one else and his illness was long."

"I know. You were wonderful. But you've never had to pinch and scrape."

"I'll have to now."

"Not through me, you won't. I wouldn't be so selfish as to make you."

She felt a sickening thrust of fear as he continued persuasively, "You'll be all right, Lesley. You'll have your father's life insurance. How much was it, by the way?"

"Nothing. He turned the policy in a long time ago in exchange for a loan."

"So it *is* true! I'd heard rumours, but didn't believe them. Good grief, what did *he* need a loan for? How did he live at a standard like this, if he needed money? How did he own such an apartment and travel in luxury—?"

"He rarely travelled."

"But when I met you, on board the *Monarch*, you both had expensive suites."

"Thanks to Uncle Barney. That cruise was his twenty-first present to me, but also to give Father the benefit of a sea voyage. His health was beginning to break. And this flat belongs to Uncle Barney, too. He's the most generous man alive and when Mother died he lent it to Father because the old place held too many reminders of her." Lesley's mouth curved indulgently. "Father being Father, he just forgot to move out."

Colin Butler said quickly, "He's your godfather too, isn't he, your Uncle Barney?"

"Yes."

"Then surely, at a time like this, he'd want to help you?"

"He offered to only this morning, after the family

6

solicitor had gone into things, but I knew you would be too proud to let me accept. I told him so."

Colin answered so quickly that she knew she must have imagined that barely perceptible pause, "That's absolutely right, darling, but we've got to be sensible and face facts. Everythnig has changed. That's why I'm doing this—"

"Doing – waht?"

"Giving you up. My sweet, don't look like that! How do you think *I* am feeling? How does any man feel when giving up the girl he loves so that she can marry some-one richer?"

She answered tensely, "I've already told you – I don't want anyone richer! I want the sort of home we can afford, together, and I want to work for it."

With elaborate patience he answered, "You'd never stand up to it, believe me. The drudgery of nursing would wear you out. Looking after one patient can't be compared with foot-slogging on the wards. And do you think *I*'d be happy, watching you trying to cope with the additional drudgery of housework? As you said – I have my pride."

"People in love can't afford pride."

"That sounds beautiful, but it isn't practical. If I gave in, I know what would happen. You'd become a worn-out drudge, penned in some dreary little suburban flat and lonely every time I went away. And now I'm going on the Caribbean run, from Miami to Puerto Rico and then on to the Virgin Islands and Martinique, and after that to the Netherland Antilles, Jamaica, and Haiti before returning to Miami. There's only a twenty-four-hour turn-round between cruises, so I'll be away for weeks at a stretch. The next one will be even longer, because this time we start from Southampton and take in New York before going on to Florida to start the

7

West Indian cruise with stop-offs at Puerto Rico and Venezuela and the Virgin Islands, as well as Jamaica and Haiti and Curaçao — and oh yes, Martinique as well. Unfortunately I can't take a wife with me, so you'd be stuck at home on your own for weeks on end, waiting for me to return. We would have no home life at all." He kissed her tenderly on the forehead. It was almost a paternal farewell. "Believe me, darling, if you marry someone better heeled than I am, I won't hold it against you."

The catch in his voice seemed very real.

She cried, "Why, you don't know me at all! I'm not afraid to face up to reality and I'll prove it to you somehow."

She clung to him then, begging, pleading, unheedful of the tears which flowed unchecked.

"We'll see, my love. My dear love. That is what you are and what you will always be, and that is why I want only your happiness and why I am doing this. Remember that, Lesley. Remember that, and don't think too harshly of me."

It was over so quickly and now he had gone, leaving the echo of his words whispering through her mind like a chill wind. The ache in her heart was even more poignant than the memory of her father, who had died with the old familiar tenderness lingering on his face, the tenderness he had always shown for her mother and herself. Simon Owen had died happy because he knew his daughter had Colin Butler to look after her, so this whole thing – Colin walking out of her life like this, calling their marriage off – was nothing but a nightmare.

The shrill insistence of the telephone cut into her thoughts, jerking her back to reality; to the luxurious room with its costly furnishings, its paintings, porcelain, and precious silver; all the treasures which her father had collected and which would now have to go to meet the heavy debts he had left behind. But she couldn't condemn him for that. Her dear, vague, irresponsible father had probably been unaware of them.

She had cause to bless him now for his passionate collecting. Uncle Barney had told her only this morning that these treasures would fetch good prices at Sotheby's. "And you still have me to count on, remember that."

He was a kindly man – Barnet Owen, Chairman of the Owen Shipping Line. As a child she had called him Uncle Bear, because he was big and burly and bluff; a bear of a man with a gentle paw and a big heart. Colin had been wrong when he once called him "a tough old nut, too hard to crack".

The relentless summons of the telephone went on, as if refusing to accept that she was not at home. She picked up the receiver and, just as if he had been summoned by the power of thought, she heard her uncle's voice echoing down the line.

"Lesley, my child, how about joining me for lunch?"

It was the calm, sane note in it that made her realise that this moment was real, and so had been those moments with Colin. They had been no part of a nightmare, after all.

She tried to answer normally, but her mind still felt stunned. Later, she thought remotely, I will think it all out. I'll go over it, word by word. I'll see everything through Colin's eyes and then I'll understand why he had to do it and I won't feel hurt any more. It isn't easy to make sacrifices for other people, and I'll never forget the unhappiness in his eyes when he went away . . .

"Lesley, are you there?"

"Yes – I'm here, Uncle Bear."

"I said how about lunch, my dear."

9

"I – I'm not hungry—"

There was a brief silence, as if her uncle were listening, trying to catch the undertones of her voice. Then he said bluntly, "Listen to me, girl – go and pretty yourself up. That session with the solicitor was tiring and depressing, and it won't do you any good to stay at home brooding on things. Put on your brightest dress – your father would like that. How about the red one he was so fond of?"

(*Oh, no – not that! Colin loved it too . . .*)

"I'll pick you up in half an hour."

The line cleared. Her uncle had gone, giving her no time for protest or argument. And it was then that she remembered the reason for Colin's visit – he, too, had called to take her out to lunch following her session with Joseph Bellamy, the family solicitor. He had telephoned before her uncle had brought the man along early that morning. Uncle Barney had arranged things that way to spare her the formality of a meeting in a chilling legal office, and then he had driven Joseph Bellamy back to his chambers, leaving her alone in the lovely Belgravia flat, comforted by the thought that despite the bad news the solicitor had brought, Colin would soon arrive to comfort her.

"We can talk about the future, darling – that will cheer you up." Those were his words when he telephoned not fifteen minutes before her uncle and Joseph Bellamy had arrived. Now she wanted to laugh hysterically. Oh yes, they had talked about the future! But not in the way she had expected.

How had it all gone awry?

Over lunch, Barney Owen studied his niece. He didn't like the taut expression about her mouth, or the stunned look in her eyes. He didn't like her silence, either. She was usually very relaxed with him because there was a bond of affection between them which, on his side, was especially deep, though she would never know the reason for that. It was a secret which went back to the days before she was born.

"You've been quick, coming back from the City in half an hour, Uncle Barney."

He could tell that it was an effort for her to make conversation, and his concern deepened. She had been on his mind ever since that interview with Bellamy, for although he'd had a pretty shrewd idea of the state of his brother's affairs, the truth had been rather worse than he imagined. Poor old Simon, he thought; he never was a business man, but he knew greater happiness in life than I've ever known despite my success. He got the one thing I wanted most, the one woman I wanted most.

His thoughts switched back to his niece, who grew more heart-rendingly like her mother every day, which was why he was particularly sensitive to her moods and emotions. He guessed now that she was trying to cover some inner distress; there was a stunned quality about her which had nothing to do with her father's death and which had not been there when he and the solicitor parted from her this morning. She had accepted her reduced circumstances philosophically. "It doesn't matter," she had said. "I am going to marry Colin. We'll have our own home. I shan't miss any of this." With a sweeping gesture she had indicated the elegant flat and all it contained.

Perhaps, thought Barney Owen, he had been tactless to say, "And what sort of a home can Colin Butler give you? Don't think I'm deriding him when I say that although he may be lucky enough to travel to America and other places on a good expense account, his position isn't all that great."

He could still see the proud tilt of her head as she answered, "He isn't going to remain where he is, Uncle Barney. I'm sure of that."

So was he. If there was one thing Barney Owen did recognise about young Colin Butler, it was his ambition.

"I didn't come from the City," he said now, belatedly. "After dropping Bellamy in Lincoln's Inn I went on to Cockspur Street. Bookings are heavy. Deciding to do the transatlantic run as well as Caribbean cruises was a wise decision. More and more people are eager to do the crossing that way and make a holiday of it."

"The *Regina* sails on the twenty-third, doesn't she?"

She knew that because Colin would be on it, and she was determined that she would be, too.

Something in her voice made her uncle glance at her from beneath his bushy eyebrows, and what he saw distressed him. There was a pallor about her which could be due to more than recent strain. He gave a shrewd guess that Colin Butler had hurt her in some way. On top of her father's death and the subsequent shock regarding the state of his affairs, that was unforgivable, but not surprising. His own interests would always come first with Colin Butler, and it wouldn't be in his own interests to marry a girl who wasn't the wealthy catch he had believed when he met her aboard the *Monarch* on that memorable trip – the daughter of Simon Owen who, everyone thought, owned that lovely place in Belgravia, and niece of Barnet Owen, head of the shipping line. Butler had rushed the girl off her feet, her uncle recalled. What had he done to her now?

But he was wise enough to ask no questions. In time, perhaps, she would talk; if not, he would just have to go on guessing. She knew he wanted to help her, he had already stressed that, but all she would accept were a few of her father's personal possessions which he had offered to buy from the estate as a wedding gift. The flat she had refused. Colin wouldn't want it, she had said. He would be too proud to accept it. He would want to provide their home himself, because he was that kind of man.

And she really believed it, the old man thought pityingly.

Suddenly Lesley said, "Uncle Bear – you meant it, didn't you, when you insisted that if I changed my mind about accepting your help, I should let you know?"

"I did indeed."

"Well – I have changed it. There is a way you can help me."

"Name it."

She took a deep breath.

"I want a job aboard the *Regina* on her next trip."

CHAPTER TWO

NORMALLY it took a great deal to surprise Barnet Owen.

"But I thought you were getting married! To Colin Butler . . ."

"Oh, I am! But not immediately. Because there isn't time – I mean, it would all be such a rush, in less than three weeks, and then he would be gone. So we decided it would really be better to wait until he comes back and I – I could look around for a little flat in the meantime."

"You could hardly do that if you were aboard the *Regina*."

She bit her lip.

"No – but I'd be with him. We could see each other every day."

"That depends on what sort of job you had, my dear. Ship's personnel rarely mix with the passengers, contrary to common belief."

"*Please*, Uncle Bear!"

His blunt features crinkled in a smile. The old, childish pet name never failed to touch his heart. He looked at her young face – yes, it was indeed a replica of her mother's – and knew that he could refuse her nothing. Whatever the motive behind this surprising request, he had to help her. Besides, that desperate pleading in her eyes was impossible to resist.

"My dear, what could you do?"

"Anything! A stewardess, perhaps . . ."

He smiled a little wryly.

"Do you know what sort of a job that is? And as a

stewardess you would see nothing of your young man. You would be below decks constantly and confined to stewards' recreational quarters – which means an area well away from the passengers – when off duty. Besides, the waiting list for stewardesses is always full; I couldn't jump it, even for you. You have no idea how many women fancy jobs on luxury liners, however menial. For the Purser's office you don't hold the necessary qualifications, so that's out, too."

"I have nursing qualifications! Parts one and two of the Central Midwive's Board, and three years training at St. Joseph's. If a reference is needed, the hospital would supply one."

"We'll go into all that, my dear. The maternity qualification is an essential, so it's lucky you hold it. Usually a vessel carries only a nursing sister besides the ship's doctor, plus a medical attendant – male – to clean and look after the surgery. However, the *Regina* does need more since her medical quarters have been enlarged. This has proved necessary because of these longer trips. The majority of passengers book for the entire cruise, but a number book only as far as New York; others come aboard there and disembark in Miami or elsewhere. So we have a continuous flow of new passengers and consequently an endless variety of medical needs to attend to. I'll tell you what I'll do – I'll put your name forward to Medical Appointments. Better still, I'll take you along this afternoon and see what we can fix up. Hey there, why are you crying into your coffee?"

"Because I'm so grateful to you, so terribly grateful!"

"It isn't settled yet, my dear. And I hope you won't weep even more when it is. I have an idea that life under Mike Halliday won't be a bed of roses."

"Who is he?"

"Ship's doctor. And a good one. Too good to be content for ever with a life on the ocean wave. He is doing the job for experience, and doing it well. But he's not an easy man. Sister Collard is the only nurse who has survived more than one voyage with him and that, I suspect, is because she's middle-aged and tough – and because she's the only woman he can tolerate."

"He sounds disagreeable," Lesley commented indifferently. She wasn't interested in Dr. Halliday. Their association would be a professional one, nothing more, so it didn't matter what he was like personally. All that did matter was being near Colin; seeing him whenever possible, proving to him that she wasn't the useless lily of the field he believed, and convincing him that two people could marry on nothing but love and work together for the material things, the things he apparently thought so important. That had come as a surprise to her; she had never imagined there was a materialistic side to his nature and she squashed the thought now. He was practical, not materialistic. A man had to be practical . . .

Her uncle's kindly voice continued, "Does Colin know of this scheme of yours?"

"No. I want to surprise him."

"A very pleasant surprise," he commented drily.

Lesley looked at her uncle with quick suspicion. Was there a cynical note in his voice? As always, she was swift in Colin's defence. Too often, she felt, this successful uncle of hers was unjust to him. Not that he ever disparaged him openly; it was just a tone of voice, an implication, even a mere tilt of an eyebrow at the mention of his name. She told herself that it was all her imagination, but it troubled her even so.

She said slowly, "Sometimes I wonder if you really like Colin."

16

"You mustn't wonder anything of the kind. He is a very able young man and I'm confident he will get just what he wants from life."

Even that, spoken in her uncle's driest tones, didn't sound particularly complimentary.

Driving towards Fenchurch Street, where the Owen Shipping Line had its City headquarters, he noticed that an air of excitement had replaced her earlier despondency, and again he wondered just what had caused this sudden change in her plans. Suspicion loomed. He was ready to take a level bet that the ambitious Colin Butler had broken the engagement on hearing the solicitor's news, but had done it in a way which gave her no reason to doubt his motives or even his love. Lesley had too much pride to chase an unwilling suitor, no matter how desperately she wanted him, but it seemed obvious that Butler had wriggled out of a position which could prove burdensome, and done it in such a way that her belief in him was unshaken.

For one angry moment, Barnet Owen longed to get his hands on the young man's neck, then the urge was replaced by one of calm resolution. There was only one way to cure his niece of her infatuation, only one way to make her see the man as he was, and that was to follow the course she wanted. As a member of the ship's crew, not as a wealthy and indulged passenger this time, she couldn't fail to observe the pattern of his behaviour. And that behaviour would undoubtedly be the same as before.

Sister Collard looked at the girl before her and thought: I knew it – pretty and useless! Everything about her suggested a cosseted background which had ill equipped her for the rigours of a nurse's life. Her Purdy haircut must have been done by a fashionable hairdresser and her make-up, subtle enough to be unobtrusive, could surely have been achieved only by the best, and therefore the most costly cosmetics. Maude Collard smothered a sigh of envy and wished she could dislike the girl, but how could one resent those large grey eyes, with their frank and open look, the shining blonde hair which swung in a neat straight cap with every turn of her head, the wide mouth which betokened generosity, and the short straight nose which completed an essentially modern and wholly likeable face? She was everything Maude would have wished to be when young, and everything she would have liked to have had in a daughter – slim, with long legs and narrow hips and the coltish grace of youth; oval chin and widely-spaced eyes; and, more than all, a complete lack of self-consciousness. That came from poise and confidence, of course. The spoilt niece of our indulgent Chairman, full of romantic ideas about life at sea. The poor kid, she'll hit the deck with a bump once the novelty wears off. And I suppose *I* will be the one to pick up the pieces.

She smothered a sigh, observing the girl's well-manicured hands and general air of ease; a girl accustomed to luxury, that was obvious. She would be a nuisance in Sick Bay, but they would just have to put up with her somehow. Not that Doc Halliday would do that with any willingness. He was already dead set against having her.

Aware of a sudden pity, the woman smiled at Lesley. Little did the girl know what she was in for! Any cherished ideas of a shipboard job being glamorous and exciting were in for a nasty jolt. But at least she had some qualifications and experience, so she should be able to cope with routine nursing.

"You've settled in your quarters, Nurse?"

"Almost, thank you, Sister."

"You like your cabin?"

"Very much."

"It's adequate, at least, and comfortable. As Personnel we are not given the best. Did you expect it?"

"I hadn't even thought about it, Sister."

The surgery door opened and a man entered. He wore the uniform of Ship's Doctor and for a moment he looked across the antiseptic room with a glance so piercing that Lesley was startled. It was then that she recalled her uncle's comments about this man, and at a glance she could well believe them. There was no leniency in his face; not even friendliness. She mentally armed herself against him.

He looked her up and down, then turned to Sister.

"This, I presume, is the assistant thrust upon us by the powers-that-be?"

Lesley stiffened. She heard Sister murmuring introductions and knew that the doctor paid no more attention than she did herself. For a long moment they looked at each other, antagonism flaring between them, and in that moment Lesley saw the strong line of his jaw and the relentless determination of his mouth. She thought she had never met a man whom she disliked so much.

He was ugly, too, although she conceded that many women might find his particular type of cragginess attractive. But not she. And those rugged features were not redeemed by their expression, which was wholly unwelcoming.

She stood there calmly, refusing to be intimidated. Sister Collard looked from one to the other, then tactfully withdrew.

Mike Halliday removed his peaked cap, revealing a broad and intelligent forehead. His nose was strong and aquiline. If that face could ever relax in a smile, it might even be human, Lesley reflected.

A full minute passed, during which he picked up some mail from his desk and glanced through it, apparently forgetting her. Was he doing this deliberately? Was he trying to make her feel uncomfortable? And if she dared to fidget, what would he do – bark at her in his deep voice, or crush her with a glance?

She waited, feeling a gathering discomfort and praying that it did not show. Instinct told her that nothing would please this man more.

Suddenly he looked up, his penetrating eyes surveying her coolly.

"Well, Nurse – and what is your first impression of this floating hotel? From the angle of the crew, I mean, not of the idle rich."

"Never having been idle, and being far from rich, I am not in a position to judge."

His eyebrows rose. She saw that his eyes were deep-set and of an attractive grey. *Attractive*? Nothing about this detestable man could possibly be attractive!

He leaned against his desk, folded his arms and said caustically, "Let's understand each other from the start. I'll begin by telling you that I don't want you here."

"You've made that very plain already."

"Then let me also make it plain that I have only accepted you because I had orders to. Orders from a high level – the Chairman of the Line, your uncle, whose influence you obviously traded upon to satisfy a whim."

"*A whim*!"

"Yes, Nurse – a whim. I know why you are here; because you think it will be fun to play at nursing on a luxury liner which might even produce a rich husband. You're in for a shock, my girl – the Atlantic crossing is romantic for the passengers, but not for personnel. And especially not in Sick Bay."

She looked up at him, and hated him. He returned the look, with a mixture of amusement and contempt. It was open warfare between them.

CHAPTER THREE

DOCTOR HALLIDAY dismissed the new nurse with a brief nod.

"You'll take your orders from Sister. You will find her outside on the ward. It's a small ward, so try not to get in the way. Especially mine."

"Gladly, sir!"

Cheeks aflame, she departed. For a moment the man looked at the closed door, then he shrugged, turned back to his letters, and forgot her.

But Lesley couldn't forget him. She was too angry. Her uncle had said that working for this man wouldn't be a bed of roses, and he was certainly right. It would be stinging nettles all the way.

Sister Collard regarded the girl with a certain sympathy. She knew only too well how caustic the doctor's tongue could be, and how disconcerting to anyone unprepared for it. In this instance he had obviously given it full vent. He had done the same when hearing of the girl's appointment, fully expecting to be saddled with an empty-headed incompetent.

"It will be worse for you than for me, Sister, because you will have to cope with her."

"I dare say I shall manage, Doctor."

And I dare say I will, she thought now, looking at Lesley's flushed face – a face which seemed surprisingly vulnerable for a young woman accustomed to having her own way. "You mark my words," Mike Halliday had said, "she'll be some spoilt brat whose every whim has

22

been indulged by a doting family. Heaven protect me from her. If heaven won't, *you* will have to."

Maude Collard had to admit that she had felt much the same way until the girl's qualifications came through. They were an agreeable surprise, and St. Joseph's had spoken well of her, but all Doctor Halliday had said then was, "Well, that's something to be thankful for, at least, but I dare say we could have found a dozen other girls with even better qualifications."

He was obviously not prepared to meet the Chairman's favoured niece even half way, or to give her one scrap of credit.

"You've met Walker, our medical orderly, haven't you, Nurse?"

Sister presented a little man clad in a white overall. He looked up from the sterilizer and nodded cheerfully. His hands were encased in rubber gloves and he continued to place surgical instruments into the unit whilst surveying the neat figure of the new nurse. He was a man without prejudices; as he frequently announced, he was "agin nobody". All he cared about was the smooth running of Sick Bay and if an addition to the staff served to increase that efficiency and lessen his own responsibilities, which had mounted with the recent growth of the ship's medical quarters, he was only too glad to welcome them.

Especially someone young and pretty, his admiring glance said. He liked the clean, wholesome look of her – and he had a weakness for blondes. Especially today's blondes. In his younger days girls were only considered pretty if their hair curled, whether blonde, brunette, or redhead. His mother and sisters and, later, his wife, had saved every spare penny for perms, and the result was usually a dull looking mop which no man yearned to touch – but looking at the shining smoothness of this

23

girl's straight hair made him want to stroke it. It was like silk. And as for her wide, friendly smile, it did his heart good. Having her around was going to make his job ten times more congenial.

It was Walker's task to clean and attend to the surgery and Sick Bay, to keep and check supplies, and to act as male nurse when needed. He was a friendly little Cockney, with a large family in Streatham and a wanderlust which prevented him from ever settling in a shore job. But there was another factor which bound him to the *Regina* – his admiration for, and loyalty to, Dr. Halliday. This devotion had been kindled at the doctor's training hospital, where Walker had been employed. It had been the most natural thing in the world to follow the man to sea. Why? Walker would echo if anyone asked such a question. Because he was a doctor worth working for, and could there be any reason better than that?

"Been tearing a strip off you, has he, Nurse?" The man's birdlike eyes twinkled sympathetically. "Don't let that worry you. There's got to be a first time and it certainly won't be the last, will it, Sister?"

Maude Collard pretended not to hear. Teaching Walker to restrain his tongue was an achievement of which she sometimes despaired. She spent the rest of the afternoon showing Lesley the ropes, finally taking her up on deck to watch the ship cast off – a manoeuvre of which Sister never tired. Leaning on the rail she said, "I'm always amazed at the way those little tugs edge a monster like this out of harbour, like pilot fish towing a whale."

In the interest and excitement of departure Lesley forgot the tyrannical doctor until she heard his voice saying in amused indulgence, "I thought you would be up here, Sister. You wouldn't miss this for anything, would you?"

Lesley was surprised to see that a corner of his mouth actually tilted in a smile as he looked down on the stout little woman.

Sister Collard chuckled.

"You're right, Doctor. I was just telling Nurse Owen how it fascinates me."

The doctor glanced at Lesley briefly. The girl wasn't even watching the busy little tugs; she was scanning the decks, obviously studying the passengers who lined the rails, her eyes searching with an eagerness he could not miss. So she was speculating already, was she? Earmarking the most attractive men, no doubt.

Now she turned and looked at him, and the eagerness in her face vanished. Her back stiffened and the reaction pleased him because it revealed that she was conscious of his disapproval, which meant that she would take good care to cross his path as little as possible, and that pleased him too.

She was staring straight ahead now, at the rapidly vanishing docks of Southampton and the green countryside beyond. What do we want a girl like this aboard for, he thought – pretty and useless and vain as a peacock, no doubt. Sister and Walker and myself could have managed as well as ever, just the three of us.

He said, "Have you seen the passenger list, Sister? If so, you'll have noticed that we have Lady Travitt on board again."

"I have noticed," Maude Collard admitted drily. "That means we'll be kept busy humouring her and listening to her gossip. I wonder who she'll find to spread scandal about this time. And, poor lonely old thing that she is, I never have the heart not to listen . . ."

"Delegate your assistant. I'm sure Miss Owen would enjoy it."

The girl's expression didn't even flicker. If she had

heard what he said, it meant nothing to her. But then, he thought with some amusement, she didn't know Lady Travitt – yet.

"Well," said Sister briskly, "I must get below. You can take an hour off to finish unpacking, Nurse, but you'll be on duty after that until eight. Then Walker will take over. Someone has to be on call round the clock. We've two mild cases of measles and mumps aboard, not yet out of quarantine but very nearly. Naturally, they went straight to Sick Bay. They're in Isolation Ward, of course."

The plump figure departed, casting a brief and eloquent glance at the doctor, who returned it blandly, deliberately refusing to catch her meaning. His remark about delegating the girl to the garrulous old Lady Travitt had been a little too pointed, even for him. He certainly seemed to have taken an unfortunate dislike to Lesley Owen – a dislike which seemed to be even greater than his earlier prejudice, as if meeting her had increased, rather than diminished, his antipathy. Sister Collard sighed. The girl seemed a nice little thing, and since they had to accept her, it would make things easier all round if they did so with good grace.

The passengers were beginning to drift below, but a few lingered on deck. Lesley's eyes scanned them swiftly, but there was no sign of Colin. He could be anywhere in this vast ship, with its twelve miles of decks and its endless public rooms. He was possibly in his stateroom unpacking, or having tea in the first-class lounge, or even exploring the ship, as passengers did when they came aboard no matter how many times they had travelled on her before, admiring the ballroom and gymnasium, the vast enclosed swimming pool which supplemented the open-air one on deck, the library and smoking room and games room, the Verandah Grill and innumerable terraces and bars. In his capacity as travel courier he could even be showing some of his firm's clients over the vessel, so there was always the likelihood of bumping into him unexpectedly. Her heart quickened at the thought of coming face to face with him, and seeing his surprise and delight.

"Looking for someone, Nurse?"

Of course, it had to be the doctor. He was still there, watching her. "If you really want to vet the passengers," he continued, "I suggest you persuade someone on the Purser's staff to take you to the Verandah Grill tonight. That is where everybody who *is* anybody congregates to dance at midnight. You can't go alone, but I've no doubt you could find an escort. Once there, selection should be quite good. The wealthy and the famous travel on the *Regina*, as I'm sure you know. As a preliminary, you could examine the passenger list and pick out a few."

He was the rudest, most detestable, most outrageous man she had ever met, and the most infuriating thing about him was his ability to leave her bereft of words.

Even more galling was the knowledge that her discomfort amused him. She could feel his eyes watching her with scorn as she struggled to find an answer and failed. In an excess of humiliation she hurried down the nearest companionway, diving into a maze of thickly-carpeted corridors in a vain search for her cabin.

Colin was aware of the familiar sense of excitement which always seized him when the great liner was finally under way; a sense of anticipation which rarely let him down. It was particularly strong today. He felt like a man released from ties, free to do what he wished whenever he wished and with whom he wished. It was a consoling feeling when a man had recently parted from someone he loved – and, of course, he did love Lesley as much as ever. Self-righteously, he had convinced himself of that, insisting in his own mind that the sacrifice he had made was indeed a sacrifice, and as confirmation he had sent her a tender little note of farewell, with a touch of martyrdom about it which he had fully expected to be reciprocated with tearful protestations. That kind of thing flattered a man's ego even when he didn't really need it.

So he had felt let down when no letter from her awaited him on the *Regina*. Poor little Lesley, he thought. She had taken it badly, but she would get over it in time. There was no need to feel conscience-stricken over what he had done. And besides, old Barney Owen was still her godfather – uncomfortable and disconcerting as the old man was. Colin didn't like Barney Owen because he knew full well that the old man disliked him in return. He had never been able to make the slightest impression on the shipowner, which was unfortunate, and not a little surprising because Colin was successful with most people. He had been successful with Lesley's father – the charming, vague, artistic man who had deceived everyone into believing him to be rich. What a defrauded feeling it had been, discovering the truth!

But there was still that lovely flat in Belgravia. A home like that was worth having, and it had been natural to assume that Lesley would inherit it. She might do so still, of course, although it would be years before hale and hearty Barney Owen died. Why the devil couldn't the man be generous enough to give it to her now, just as it stood? He didn't need it for himself. He had a fine house in Regent's Park, so he could have given the Belgravia home to them as a wedding gift without even missing it.

What sort of help *had* the man offered her? Lesley hadn't said; merely that she had declined it because she knew that he, Colin, would be too proud to let her accept . . . which, he assured himself with pious haste, he would have been, of course.

All the same, it would be nice to know just what Barnet Owen's offer *had* consisted of. It wasn't pleasant, being troubled by the vague fear that perhaps he had been too precipitate in giving Lesley up, that it might have been wiser to wait – but for what? For the results of an auction at Sotheby's which would only clear a mountain of debts? Colin Butler gave himself a mental shake and turned to the future. A man had to think of the future . . .

Before leaving his stateroom he scanned the passenger list. It was part of his job to study this with an eye to contacts. The only pages he skipped were those listing ship's personnel.

As always, there was the usual quota of celebrities, titles, and millionaires whose names were well known to an envious public. There were plenty of unknown names, too, but all were no doubt equally rich or successful. They wouldn't be taking trips like this otherwise. After calling at New York, the *Regina* was going on to Miami, then to San Juan, the capital of Puerto Rico, then to St. Thomas in the U.S. Virgin Islands, and after that to Fort de France in Martinique, Caracas in Venezuela, Aruba in the Dutch Antilles and the Dutch port of Willemstad in Curaçao, before proceeding to Port Antonio in Jamaica and finally to Port-au-Prince in Haiti before returning to Miami – one had to have money for cruises like this and he would soon weed out those who, like himself, were travelling on expense accounts. He had learned to detect them at a glance, just as he had learned to assess the daughters of rich Americans, or women to whom he knew, without vanity, he would appeal, be they wives or mothers. He had made many a successful contact through scraping acquaintance with women that way, either on deck, in the swimming pool, or on the ballroom floor. He had met Lesley that way, and he remembered the meeting with nostalgic regret.

The future, he resolved – I must think of the future! And since it no longer included Lesley, the best thing to do was to forget her.

He was doing that very successfully as he scanned the first-class lounge where afternoon tea was now being served. There were many interesting groups and his eye ran over them swiftly, until his attention was caught by a girl sitting alone. Young, unescorted, and quite ravishingly pretty. She was also beautifully dressed, with that elegant simplicity which proclaimed money. That she should be alone seemed too good to be true.

He chose a nearby table. Not too near, but close enough to observe her, and he wasn't disappointed. Luck seemed to be favouring him. Out of the hundreds of passengers in this floating palace, he had come face to face with this one the moment they set sail! He took it as a good omen, and resolved not to lose sight of her.

She didn't spend much time over tea. When she rose he watched her walk towards the double gilt doors, then followed casually. He timed it so that he reached the doors before a hovering steward opened them for her. She looked up with a smile, thanked him, then walked towards the lifts.

She alighted at the Promenade Deck, which spoke for itself. His own accommodation was way down on B Deck, but he pretended that he was getting out here too, and followed her at a discreet distance, determined to note the number of her stateroom and check on her identity at the list posted up by the Purser's office, but a figure hurrying round a corner suddenly collided with him full tilt.

It was a girl. He steadied her, then his hands fell nervelessly from her shoulders.

"*Lesley*!"

His voice was hoarse with disbelief, and he stood there for a full moment, staring at her. Not until she laughed did he really believe she was real. It was Lesley's laugh at its happiest.

"It can't be you!" he protested.

"Touch me again, to make sure."

The dimple in her right cheek, the one he loved to kiss, deepened visibly.

"Oh, Colin, I was wondering where you were and when we would meet! I didn't dare hope it would be so soon."

"But what are you doing here – and why the uniform?" He broke off. "Good grief, you're not a stewardess, are you?"

"No, I'm a nurse. Haven't you noticed my cap? I've got a job on the medical staff."

Her smile vanished abruptly; her eyes were suddenly wary. At the far end of the corridor she glimpsed a uniformed figure – a tall, rangy figure with a craggy sort of face.

"Colin, I must go! I mustn't be seen here. I'm only allowed on these corridors in the course of duty. I was looking for staff quarters, and got lost . . ."

He caught her arm, delaying her.

"There's no one about. Tell me how you come to be here—"

"He – they – might come back. Meet me tonight, after dinner. I'll wait for you on the Boat Deck, in the stern."

"Better make it late. I'm not sure how long I'll be."

"All right. Say ten o'clock?" She cast an anxious glance down the corridor and saw to her relief that the uniformed figure had disappeared. She reached up swiftly then and kissed him. "I'll explain everything – just how it happened and why I did it, though you ought to guess that. Darling, say you're glad. Say it quickly!"

He stammered his assurances, and then she was gone. The corridor was empty again, and behind one of the solid mahogany doors the girl had vanished – the girl Lesley had made him lose sight of.

It was Sister Collard, Lesley decided, who was going to make her job bearable. She was a kindly, understanding woman beneath her brisk efficiency. Lesley knew they could work well together, and since she would come into closer contact with her than with the medical officer, there was no reason to be unduly perturbed by the doctor's attitude. Besides, he mattered little compared with Colin, from whom she had parted with a sense of happiness and anticipation. Meeting him so unexpectedly and so soon after setting sail had been lucky. She might have waited a long time before catching even a glimpse of him. The gods, she decided, must be on her side, so after finally settling into her quarters she reported for duty with a light heart.

"You'll find most of the work just normal routine nursing," Sister told her, "with occasional emergencies. Sometimes seriously ill patients come aboard whose condition bars them from flying; some take the full cruise for health reasons, others just travel from Southampton to New York – and *vice versa* – to visit specialists either in America or London. Only those under constant attention are admitted into Sick Bay, the rest are nursed in their staterooms or cabins. Doctor Halliday thinks this arrangement better for them psychologically." She added: "Don't be misled by the doctor's manner."

"Could I be?"

The wry note in Lesley's voice made the woman smile.

"You could, indeed. He's a fine doctor, and a humane one."

"I'll credit his medical skill since you vouch for it, but as for his humane side, I'll believe in that when I sample it."

Sister said in a tone of reproof, "You must understand that Doctor Halliday is a most fair-minded man who dislikes favouritism of any kind, so you are starting at a disadvantage. It will be harder for you than an ordinary nurse."

"I am an ordinary nurse."

"Not to him. You are the favoured niece of the company's Chairman."

"And therefore he considers me useless and incompetent! I hope you don't share his views, Sister."

"That's up to you, my dear. All I want you to do is prove your competence."

"I shall do my best – but may I ask you something? Did *you* not want me aboard, either?"

"I can't deny I was against your appointment. That was inevitable. No ordinary staff member takes kindly to the idea of some – shall we say favoured? – person joining it."

"My uncle made it quite clear that working for Doctor Halliday was not exactly being 'favoured'. He warned me about him."

"Did he, indeed?" Sister spoke with some asperity. "Well, I suppose the doctor's reputation is well earned, up to a point, but he's a good doctor, all the same. Some time you might take the trouble to let your uncle know that."

"There won't be any need. He told me so himself."

Sister's glance softened. She felt rather sorry for this girl, because her uncle had done her no great favour in bringing her into Mike Halliday's service. There were other ships' doctors who would have treated a girl in her position with considerably more tact, even friendliness. As it was, she had won this particular doctor's antagonism even before arrival, so she was starting off against greater odds than a girl who had landed the job without any string-pulling.

It had even made no difference when Sister herself had pointed out that there actually wasn't another nurse, holding the necessary qualifications, applying for an appointment at that precise moment, and that if this girl hadn't turned up they would have had to contact the usual agencies and search for the right one – so why shouldn't Lesley Owen be given a chance, since she filled the bill? When Mike's back was up, trying to reason with him was useless. To his way of thinking, a principle was a principle, and no amount of argument could have the slightest effect once his mind was made up.

Stubborn? Of course he was. Infuriating, too. But Sister Collard's sympathetic heart sensed an underlying unhappiness from which he only seemed to escape in work. She was confident that he could have held a good appointment ashore, but for some reason known only to himself he chose a life at sea – a life which offered little advancement, other than the remote possibility of becoming the line's Head of Medical Appointments at some vague future date, a desk job ashore which would never appeal to a man like Mike.

On the other hand, he was not the usual roving type. Many ships' doctors possessed a wanderlust which made a steady life ashore quite unacceptable. To Maude Collard's mind, Mike Halliday was the type to be in country practice, a family practice; a man who should marry and settle down and find happiness and fulfilment with a wife and children, and work he loved.

Sometimes she felt that he was trying to escape from

some emotional problem, or a disappointment which went deep. Or maybe only from himself . . .

A telephone on the surgery wall buzzed discreetly. Sister jerked away from the problem of Doctor Halliday and Nurse Owen and the worry as to how they were going to get along. They would have to work out their own salvations; she had her work to think of. Her own problems, too – an ageing mother in a bungalow at Shoreham, who was beginning to need her daughter's constant care. But Maude Collard had spent her nursing career at sea and, if she left the Line prematurely, her annuity from the pension scheme would drop accordingly. She couldn't afford that – but neither could she afford to pay someone else to nurse her mother.

The world was a difficult place, she reflected with a sigh as she picked up the telephone receiver.

"As I thought," she said to Lesley as she hung up. "Lady Travitt. Come along, my dear – she's your patient from now on and I hand her to you gladly!" As they hurried on their way she continued, "The old lady is a diabetic and needs regular doses of insulin. It will be your job to give them to her daily."

Lady Travitt was garrulous, elderly, and promised to be more than trying. She was also over-dressed, over-bejewelled, and over made-up. She occupied one of the most expensive suites on the *Regina* and created a scene at the Purser's office should she ever be given anything but her favourite one on the Promenade Deck. She bullied the stewardesses, snapped the heads off the dining room stewards, and reprimanded any passenger who dared to place his deck chair in the spot which she regarded as exclusively her own. She complained about everything, praised nothing, and constantly threatened that she would never travel on the *Regina* again.

She was autocratic and frequently rude. She considered no one's feelings. When in New York she compared it unfavourably with London, and when in London insisted that the place lagged behind New York. Nothing, and no one, ever seemed to please her – yet people tolerated her and even liked her. The crew accepted her abuse uncomplainingly, partly because she tipped generously, and partly because they also pitied her, although if questioned none would have been able to say just why. She was rich enough to enjoy a life of ease and comfort and self-indulgence. She appeared to have everything to make her happy.

And yet the first thing Lesley noticed was the guarded expression of her eyes, as if she were determined to allow no one a glimpse of her heart. And the second thing was the tight line of her mouth, as if she were afraid that, if permitted to relax, it would betray her. What would it do – droop pathetically; reveal a sadness she was too proud to acknowledge?

"Ah, there you are, Sister! I must say I'm glad you're still with the *Regina* – I've got used to you. The moment they transfer you to another vessel, let me know. I've made it perfectly clear that I won't be nursed by anyone but you, and I'll sue the Owen Shipping Line if I ever come aboard and find you're not here. Make a note of that, and if they ever decide to post you to another ship, tell 'em *I* must be consulted." The sharp eyes turned to Lesley. "And who is this?"

Maude Collard answered smoothly, "This is Nurse Owen. I have brought her along to meet you."

"Why? *I* don't want her. Send her away."

"When she has given you your injection."

"*What?*" the old lady screeched. "That's your job, Sister. I won't be attended by a slip of a girl I don't even know!"

"You will get to know her, Lady Travitt, and you will get along well together, I'm sure."

"Well, *I* am not. Send her away, I tell you."

Sister smiled and pretended not to hear.

"That's a very pretty blouse you're wearing. Rolling up the sleeve won't crease it, I hope?"

"Would I be likely to wear something which wouldn't stand up to this tiresome injection business?" the old lady snapped.

"Of course not. You're much too sensible." Sister's eyes signalled to Lesley. "Ah, that's right, Nurse. You see, Lady Travitt, Nurse Owen knows how to handle lovely silk like that."

The old lady looked at her bare arm with surprise. She had been quite unaware of Lesley's fingers deftly preparing it for the hypodermic.

Lesley smiled down at her.

"From Thailand, isn't it?" she said.

Elvira Travitt sniffed.

"So you've nursed some well-dressed patients in your time, have you? Not that you've had much time, from the look of you. How old are you, girl? Don't bother to tell me – if Sister is heartless enough to inflict you on me, I would rather not know how young and inexperienced you are."

"Nurse Owen is well qualified," Maude Collard assured her. "She would not be employed by the Line otherwise."

The injection was over in a moment. Sister's well-trained face gave no indication of her relief and satisfaction. This trying old woman could be handed over to the new nurse without anxiety.

For the first time that Maude Collard could remember, Elvira Travitt was lost for words. But she wasn't going to admit either surprise or gratification. She rasped instead, "Well, Sister, you can give my compliments to Doctor Halliday and tell him that although I have allowed this girl to manhandle me once, I won't a second time. So he'd better send *you* in future, and alone."

The sight of Lesley's face made Sister's heart stab. The poor kid, she thought – first Mike abuses her, and now Elvira. She telegraphed her reassurance to the girl, trying to convey without words her own satisfaction. The job couldn't have been done more competently, or with less fuss or discomfort, and well did the old lady know it.

Lesley went into the bathroom to cleanse the hypodermic. She was suddenly despondent again. If it weren't for Sister Collard, she thought unhappily, I'd be in for a pretty bad time between the doctor and this particular patient. But there would be others, of course; more appreciative ones, with luck. And what did the difficulties of the job matter so long as she was on the same vessel as Colin? The voyage wouldn't last for ever, and by the end of it she would surely have achieved her aim – to win him back.

Lady Travitt's voice came to her clearly through the open door.

"A dull lot on board, Sister. Not an interesting name on the passenger list. A few of the old regulars like myself . . ." Her cackle was dry and not without humour. "The usual stupid film stars, a bunch of social climbers, and the rest are names which mean nothing to me."

"You'll have found out everything about them, all the same, by the end of the trip. In fact, I'm quite sure you've already given the tea lounge a thorough inspection."

Sister Collard's voice was good-natured and indulgent,

so full of kindness that not even Elvira Travitt could take offence.

"There's not an interesting face amongst the lot of them – I had a good look during tea – except the little girl next door."

"And who is she?"

"I haven't had time to find out yet. But I will. A pretty girl and a nice little thing from the look of her. Of course, you can never tell – an innocent face is often a mask. Naturally, the men noticed her, especially one handsome young devil whom I've seen on these trips before—" She broke off as Nurse Owen reappeared. "You wouldn't look bad in a few pretty clothes yourself, Nurse."

"Thank you," Lesley murmured, suppressing a smile. "I have taken the trouble to bring a few with me, to wear when off duty."

"But don't forget, Sister – I won't be attended by any-one but you. Remember that."

"Myself or Nurse Owen, I promise you, Lady Travitt," Sister answered serenely. "Let us know if you want anything further, won't you?"

Quietly and quickly, she closed the stateroom door before the old lady had a chance to reply.

Outside she said, "Take no notice of her, my dear. She will come round. In a few days, if you handle her as competently as you did just now, she'll be writing to Head Office telling them that unless she is attended to exclusively by you in the future, she will never use the Line again!"

"I take it she is a regular passenger?"

"Whenever we touch New York. She has a daughter there. A lovely girl. She's married to Tad Wilmott, the American impresario, and is on the stage herself."

The door next to Lady Travitt's suite opened just as they were passing, revealing a luxurious stateroom beyond and a girl framed in the aperture – obviously the girl the old lady had been talking about. She was wearing a chic little black velvet dress which was the perfect choice for a first night at sea. Lesley received the impression of a frank young face and an air which only money could provide.

A moment later she was gone.

Maude Collard sighed. "The idle rich – how I envy 'em!"

"Why?"

"My dear girl, isn't it obvious?"

"The only obvious thing about wealth is the anxiety of keeping it and the hole it leaves when it disappears."

"And what do you know about that – you, with your connections? Frankly, I can't understand why you even *want* to work."

"Because I must, for one thing, and because I like it, for another. As for my 'connections', Sister, I'd be much happier if you forgot them. My uncle is wealthy and influential, I know, but I am not. When my father died recently I was left without a penny. That's why I'm here."

Sister's face revealed both surprise and sympathy.

"My dear, I wish I had known! Why didn't you tell us?"

"Us?"

"The doctor and myself."

Lesley answered forcefully, "I would hate Doctor Halliday to know! Promise you won't tell him, please."

"But his attitude would change, if he knew."

"I don't care about his attitude, and I don't want it to change for that reason. I want to make him eat his words by proving I am a good nurse."

She was surprised to realise how greatly she wanted that.

Maude Collard studied her carefully, then said, "Very well, my dear, I'll say nothing, but if it is any help, I'd like you to know that I am on your side."

"It does help, Sister. Thank you."

They had reached the surgery. Opening the door for Sister to pass through, Lesley saw Mike Halliday at the telephone. He was listening to someone on the end of the line and his face was set.

"All right, Lady Travitt, I'll remember – and thank you for letting me know."

Lesley walked straight through the surgery to the dispensary, closing the dividing door. She put away the insulin, sterilised her hypodermic and locked it up, trying not to remember the doctor's stern face as he replaced the receiver, nor to wonder why Lady Travitt had rung. Beyond the closed door came the murmur of voices.

"And what," Sister was saying, "was that old woman ringing about?"

"The injection Nurse Owen administered. Apparently the girl is quite incompetent, as I expected, and the old lady insists that you do it in future. You'd better keep our spoilt-little-rich-girl away from her."

"I was there when Nurse gave the injection, and I couldn't have done it better myself! Elvira Travitt is being malicious because I told her she would have to accept Nurse Owen if she was on duty when her injection was due. I have the right to delegate my assistant to any duties I believe her capable of carrying out, and that is one of them. As for being a spoilt little rich girl—"

Sister checked.

"Well – you were saying?"

"Simply that I refuse to indulge that old woman's complaints, especially when they are unjustified."

"As you say, Sister, you have complete authority on

the nursing side, but when Lady Travitt complains again, *you* can deal with her, not I."

"Gladly! But I don't imagine her complaints will continue for long."

"You don't mean to tell me that the Owen girl has won you over?"

"And why not?"

"Because girls like her are a liability, not an asset; a hindrance, not a help. I thought you were too level-headed to be influenced by who she is."

"I don't care *who* she is, Doctor. I only care *what* she is."

"And so do I! And because of what she is, she will never succeed in winning *me* over!"

CHAPTER FOUR

COLIN was waiting for Lesley on the Boat Deck. She saw the glow of his cigarette in the darkness, and the shadowy outline of his figure. He was standing beneath a davit, looking out to sea, and for a moment she watched him. There was a tension about him, a sort of waiting stillness which reflected a little of her own excitement.

All day she had longed for this moment and now it had come she felt almost breathless. She was afraid to look ahead too eagerly, yet it was impossible not to feel that this reunion was to be a momentous one. He would take her in his arms and admit that he couldn't do without her . . .

He did take her in his arms, and she was so happy to be close to him that she overlooked the automatic way in which he did it, and was quite unaware that he really didn't know how to handle the situation, or that the gesture was a sort of refuge, a stalling for time.

Like Lesley, he had had this meeting uppermost in his mind ever since they had met below decks, but for a different reason. He was afraid of it. He recognised that fact with a feeling of surprise, for he was not by nature a cowardly man. If anything, he was over-confident, and usually with very good reason. His plans rarely misfired, but he attributed this not so much to his good luck as to his own good sense.

So Lesley's unexpected appearance on the *Regina* was not only a surprise, but something to be handled carefully. Of course, he was glad to see her and, of course, she still

43

appealed to him, but he mustn't let sentiment overcome wisdom and he certainly must not be carried away by emotion.

All the same, her lips were very soft beneath his own.

He drew away resolutely. "Lesley, we've got to talk."

She laughed. He could see the happiness in her eyes and knew it would be the easiest thing in the world to throw reason overboard and simply enjoy being with her, but that, as yet, would be folly. Someone had to be practical and it obviously wasn't going to be Lesley.

"Colin, last time we met, *you* did all the talking and every word of it was wrong. I've proved it, haven't I? You thought I couldn't land a job, let alone come to grips with life. You thought I would weep a little and then console myself with someone else, but you underestimated me." There was reproach in her voice. "I honestly thought you knew me better, but apparently you didn't. But now—"

"Now you've been clever, and surprised me."

His tone was crisp, even faintly admiring, but there was an underlying note in it which dimmed her happiness.

"You don't sound too pleased."

"Of course, I'm pleased."

"Well, then, what is there to talk about, except the future? We're together again, and that is all that matters."

He asked, with the air of one indulging a stubborn child, "But what is it going to accomplish, my dear?"

"Why, I – I don't—"

"Exactly. You don't know. Nor, quite frankly, do I."

"I wasn't going to say that. The question seemed so – unnecessary."

"My sweet, I lack your ability to overlook the obvious. Wonderful as it is to be together, it doesn't make things easier. Don't look like that, darling, or I shall take

44

you in my arms and kiss you again, and then common sense won't have a chance."

"I don't want it to have a chance." The dimple at the corner of her mouth quivered provocatively. It was damned attractive, he thought, and wished she wouldn't smile at him like that. It wasn't fair of her, any more than it was fair to spring this surprise on him. If she *had* to indulge this hare-brained scheme, she might at least have given him due warning.

Resorting to criticism fostered a sense of resentment in him which, in turn, kindled a faint anger. He was glad of that, because ever since Lesley's appearance on board he had been troubled by doubt and a certain apprehension. For the first time since he had started making these trips he felt that fate was being unpredictable.

A determined line tightened his mouth. Had it *really* been an accident that brought Lesley to that particular corridor at that particular moment, just when he was following an extremely pretty girl and anticipating a new and exciting acquaintanceship, full of possibilities? Had Lesley already seen him, and followed him, deliberately forestalling that very desirable meeting?

The infuriating thing about it was that from that moment he hadn't seen the girl again. He had scanned the dining room eagerly, but it was so vast that people dining at opposite ends couldn't possibly see each other. He had found himself at a table with a couple of elderly spinsters from the Middle West, an uncommunicative German with his fat *hausfrau*, and a boring politician, with none of whom he had the slightest thing in common. If he could only discover at which table the girl was sitting, he would see what he could do about getting a transfer. After all, why shouldn't he enjoy congenial company? All too often, in the pursuit of desirable contacts, he had to suffer acute boredom, but one glance

45

at that girl had assured him that she would be not only far from boring, but very desirable indeed . . .

Eating his dinner moodily and making polite conversation with his dull dinner companions, he had even wondered whether Lesley had come on this voyage to spy on him, but a sense of guilt had overcome that thought. All the same, it was a surprising thing for her to do, and she had obviously done it solely to be near him, and wasn't that tantamount to spying?

He asked abruptly, "How did you get this job?"

"I applied for it," she said in some surprise.

"Through your uncle, I suppose."

"He passed me on to Medical Appointments, if that is what you mean. I was on my own from then on. I had to be interviewed and approved like any other applicant."

"And chance alone brought you on this ship?"

"Darling, of course not! I asked for the *Regina* particularly. Surely you're not surprised? I knew when you broke our engagement that you didn't really want to. You said as much. Well, I decided to prove that what *I* said was true also – that I wouldn't marry anyone else and was perfectly capable of working. I didn't care what sort of a job I took. As it happens, the medical quarters on this ship were recently extended and an extra nurse was needed. I had the necessary qualifications, so here I am. That's all there is to it, except that I'm glad I got the job, difficult as it is."

"Difficult?"

"Not as far as the work is concerned, but the doctor isn't an easy man to work for."

"My poor darling . . ."

Feeling faintly reassured, he put an arm about her and drew her to him. She sighed, and leaned closer.

"Oh, Colin, for one awful moment I thought you weren't glad to see me!"

46

"That's nonsense." He kissed her temple, rubbing his cheek against her soft hair. The fragrance of her came to him like a reminder of past happiness and he forgot everything but the pleasure of having her near. How damnably unfair it was that life should cheat them of so much, just on the eve of marriage! They could have been happy together in that luxury Belgravia flat . . .

He asked carefully, "Did you tell your uncle why you wanted to come on the *Regina*?"

"Of course. I told him I wanted to be near you."

"*And* what happened between us when we last met?"

"No. I told him we had decided to postpone the wedding until you returned."

"And he asked no questions?"

"Why should he?"

(Because he was always too astute, too shrewd, too watchful . . .)

Aloud, Colin said, "If he knew I had tried to give you up, your uncle wouldn't understand that I was thinking only of *your* happiness, *your* future."

She turned within the curve of his arm, and kissed him.

"It doesn't matter. Uncle Barney's a dear, but he *is* an old bachelor. Work has been his greatest love always, though sometimes I wonder why. I've always felt that at some time in his life he was deeply in love with someone, but who she was, I don't know."

Colin shrugged.

"Well, he certainly devoted himself to other things, and very successfully. I can't think what an old bachelor wants with all that wealth – even what he does with it."

"He lives comfortably. He is kind and generous to others, particularly those close to him and those who work for him. Sometimes he takes a good holiday, but not very often. He frequently took me with him when I was a child – and, of course, he was wonderful to Father, who had no business head at all, poor dear. But never mind Uncle Barney. I know you've never liked him much, but that is only because you've never known him as I do. That's why you don't understand him."

"I would understand him better if he had helped you when your father died."

"But he did!"

"In what way? Merely by buying a few of your father's cherished antiques for you?"

"It was all I would accept. That, and an introduction to the right quarter in going after this job."

"I don't suppose he was generous enough to offer you anything else."

Swiftly, defensively, Lesley said, "You're wrong! If you must know, he offered me the flat."

He was stunned into silence.

"*And* everything in it," Lesley continued. "I didn't tell you because I knew you would call it charity. Some men would let another provide their home, but I knew you better. I told him we couldn't possibly start our married life that way, and he respected me for it."

Colin was very still. He felt winded, bereft of words. From the moment he had entered that Belgravia home, he had coveted it. It was the sort of place he dreamed of owning – and Lesley had turned it down!

When he regained his breath, he asked: "What does your uncle plan to do with it?"

"I haven't the faintest idea. Sell it, probably. He owns the freehold."

(*Freehold! Ours for ever and ever! Maybe it wasn't too late . . .*)

"You know, Lesley, it was you who said that people in love can't afford pride . . ."

"I meant it, too, so you mustn't be too proud to let me

48

work. Oh, darling, you still want to marry me, don't you?"

"Of course!"

His arms went round her possessively. His kiss was so passionate that Lesley was unaware of everything but the realisation that she had won him back – and so quickly, so quickly!

She didn't hear the measured footfall on the deck. It was Colin who jerked away, swearing beneath his breath. "Turn your back, darling – whoever it is will pass in a moment." He looked down at her crisp white overall, conspicuous in the moonlight. "Why the devil didn't you change, or fling on a coat?" he whispered. "I know full well that any goings-on between ship's crew and passengers are frowned on."

She was about to answer when the footsteps stopped and a voice said, "Good evening, Nurse. Enjoying the night air?"

Over Colin's shoulder, Lesley looked into the cynical eyes of the doctor.

Colin released her abruptly.

"I'll be off," he murmured. *For your sake*, his expression said as he gave her a fleeting smile.

He was gone before she realised it, leaving her face to face with Mike Halliday.

She remarked icily, "I am off duty, Doctor."

"So it seems. But I should like to point out that you are still in uniform, and for a ship's nurse to be caught in such a position casts a bad reflection on the medical staff. If you *must* behave in such a way, kindly make sure that you draw no attention to yourself. Your uniform makes you conspicuous."

"You don't understand—"

"I understand perfectly, as I understood you on arrival. I guessed then that you were a good-time girl

49

out for all she could get. Which means a man, of course." He gave a slight bow. "Let me congratulate you. You have certainly wasted no time."

Lesley shook with anger as she went below. The man had no right to insult her. Whatever she did off duty was no concern of his.

This defiant reasoning was not helped by the knowledge that, in one respect at least, she had been at fault. She should have remembered that she was wearing her uniform and that it would be noticeable, especially against the background of a man's dark suit. Any passenger seeing her in such a compromising situation could misinterpret it. She could well imagine the raised eyebrows, the whispered comments. Such thoughts were as humiliating as the doctor's injustice. She thought bitterly that it was just like him to put the worst possible interpretation on things.

As for still being in uniform, there was good reason for that. She had had no time to change, thanks to old Lady Travitt, who had retired early but been unable to sleep. A harassed stewardess had finally pleaded with Sister for some sleeping pills. "If I don't get her off somehow, she'll be ringing that bell of hers all night!" So Sister Collard, determined to make the old lady accept the new nurse, had despatched Lesley to attend to her.

Inevitably, that had not pleased Elvira.

"So it's you again," she had snapped.

Lesley had smiled sympathetically, prepared a mild sedative, waited whilst the old lady drank it and stayed with her until she finally slept. Before the faded eyes closed they regarded the new nurse with the first flicker of friendliness. "Maybe I was wrong about you, young woman."

The moment represented a hurdle overcome and the

recollection of it soothed a little of Lesley's indignation. One of her enemies, at least, promised an earlier capitulation than she had dared to hope for, and since she had already won an ally in Sister, the disturbing doctor could be ignored.

She decided to glance at the woman before going to bed. On her way she crossed the wide foyer outside the main first-class lounge and glimpsed the well-dressed crowd within. At midnight, the more energetic amongst them would adjourn to the Verandah Grill to dance until dawn, by which time she, the ship's nurse, would be sound asleep. And Colin – what would he do? Dance for awhile, perhaps. She couldn't really be jealous if he did. Why should he cut himself off from the social life of the ship just because she couldn't share it with him?

All the same, she wished he had not beaten *quite* so hasty a retreat up there on the Boat Deck, even if he had considered it the most tactful thing to do. From her point of view, it had been the least comforting. It might have taken the wind out of Mike Halliday's sails, to be coolly confronted by a man who didn't give a damn for his opinion; even more deflating to the man's ego would have been an admission that the man making love to her was the man she was going to marry. He could hardly have accused her of light behaviour then. As soon as she saw Colin again, she would persuade him that there was no need for secrecy, here on board the *Regina*, and how she would enjoy seeing the doctor's face when he heard the news!

Lady Travitt was sleeping soundly, which was a good thing because the voyage was becoming choppy and already some of the passengers were going below. Leaving the stateroom Lesley came face to face with a stewardess emerging from the next suite.

"Would you take a look at my passenger, Nurse? The

51

poor thing's so sea-sick I was coming along to the surgery for something. Nothing I've given her so far has made any difference."

The girl was in bed, white and exhausted. She gave Lesley a wan smile. Even at a moment like this she caught the eye. She had a piquant little face, but one which was elevated above mere prettiness by the additional asset of lively intelligence.

But what arrested Lesley, as she stooped above the girl, was the exquisite nightdress and the matching quality of discarded underwear strewn on the floor, shed hurriedly before their owner collapsed on the bed. The clothes were new and lovely enough for a bride.

Her bout of sickness was one of those short, sharp attacks which would probably clear as suddenly. "You'll be all right soon," Lesley said. "Meanwhile, I'll give you something to speed the cure. Will you collect it from Dispensary in about five minutes, Stewardess? I'll look in again early tomorrow morning, Miss—?"

"Davis," the girl said weakly. "Patsy Davis."

So ordinary a name was almost an anti-climax.

Lesley picked up some of the clothing from the floor and handed it to the stewardess to put away. There was a small dressing room as part of the suite, which was one of the more expensive ones and, in itself, further evidence of the girl's means.

There was something about Patsy Davis which caught Lesley's interest.

"Is she travelling alone?" she asked the stewardess, once outside.

"Seems like it, Nurse. It's not often we have anyone like her travelling singly. Not that *she's* likely to remain single for long, I'd say!"

Lesley agreed, and promised to prepare something for the girl right away.

Approaching the dispensary, she was surprised to see a light shining beneath the surgery door and even more surprised, on opening it, to meet the ship's doctor again. He was sitting at his desk and looked up with a swift frown. At the sight of her, it became a scowl. Lesley crossed the room and entered the dispensary without a word.

She was busy at the counter which ran beneath a long range of shelves, on which stood an array of bottles, all neatly labelled with their Latin derivations. They were firmly clamped to withstand the motion of the ship, and as she took one down she was surprised by the doctor's voice again. She turned to see him leaning against the door, watching her critically, and her sudden awareness of him threatened to undermine her confidence. She had to exercise the utmost control to prevent a sudden trembling of her hands, and the reaction was so inexplicable that she was filled with surprise and shame. Why should she care if this man turned on her that mocking and ironical glance?

"You're being very diligent, Nurse. Is it designed to make a good impression on me? Do you think that by returning to the surgery when off duty you will fill me with admiration?"

Anger was a merciful safety valve. It served her well now. With a steady hand she tested the seals of the gelatine capsules she had prepared, packed them in a plastic pill container, labelled it, and answered coolly, "Since I had no idea you were here, Doctor, how could I expect to 'impress' you?"

Unexpectedly, he grinned. The sudden crinkling of his craggy features could hardly be called a smile, for there was neither gentleness in it nor good will – only a grudging amusement.

"*Touché*. That point, at least, I concede to you,

53

although you might have learned from Sister that I always return here after dinner for what I hope will be a few undisturbed hours."

"Might I suggest, sir, that you ask her whether she passed that information on to me?"

For the first time, he felt a flicker of interest in the girl. She had spirit, if nothing else. She stood up to him without insolence, answered without impertinence, and displayed a cool self-confidence which he was forced to admire. He was careful to hide his reaction, but he found himself enjoying the challenge of her.

There came a tap on the door. Lesley opened it, handed the stewardess the pills, said good night and, without another glance at the doctor, went away.

After she had gone, Mike Halliday went back to his work and took up his pen again. But he could not concentrate. His eyes wandered to the closed door and he found himself staring at it, seeing the picture of Lesley Owen framed there, trim and neat in her uniform, her hair smooth and straight beneath her cap. There was nothing spectacular about her and he had to admit that in appearance at least she wasn't the glamour-girl he had expected. But he still wished she had not come. More than that, he began to wish quite fervently that she would leave at the end of the voyage.

Who was that man she had been with, up there on the Boat Deck? The brief glimpse of his face was somehow familiar. Probably he had travelled on the *Regina* before, but Mike kept away from the passengers except in the course of doctoring them. He could have joined in the social side of the ship had he wanted to, but he had shut himself away from that sort of thing long ago. Work was his sole interest in life now, and he found it more satisfying than the company of any particular woman. He would have dined in his own quarters had it been possible, but ship's etiquette demanded otherwise. It was in the restaurant, no doubt, that he had seen Nurse Owen's companion.

He felt a sudden desire to find out more about the man, and to try to analyse why he appealed to the girl. That this appeal was great, had been obvious. He had spoken impulsively up there on the Boat Deck, and very much to his own surprise, and now regretted it, but somehow the disgust he felt (was it disgust, or anger?) had prompted him to speak without thought. But perhaps it was a good thing; to be discovered and reprimanded on her first night out might have a salutary effect. He wasn't interested in her as a person, but he *was* interested in the reputation of the medical staff as a whole. Shipboard flirtations never escaped the attention of passengers; what went on when in port was another matter, but when under way every member of the crew was responsible for preserving the dignity and respect for which all officers, from the Captain downwards, set an example.

He turned once again to his work, but it was no good; the memory of that moment when he had come across her in that man's arms kept thrusting itself into his mind. The man could have engineered the meeting himself, of course. That handsome face was enough to bowl over any girl, and Lesley Owen was probably no different from the rest. And perhaps no better than the rest. He wondered why the thought disturbed him.

On one thing he was determined – this girl's face must not be allowed to come between himself and his one chief interest in life. He had started writing this medical book during his first cruise as ship's doctor of the *Regina*, and until this moment nothing had hindered it. He picked up his pen again and began to write resolutely, but after ten minutes he knew that not a single word was satisfactory.

Furious with himself, he tore up the sheets, switched off the surgery lights, and went along to his cabin, but even as he stripped and showered, his mind was recalling that boat deck scene. The man had beaten a hasty retreat, a fact he now recalled with contempt. That proved that the incident was nothing more than a flirtation, cheap and meaningless, typical of many shipboard *affaires*. As far as the passengers went, it didn't matter what they did, but as far as the medical staff was concerned – *his* staff – the sooner Lesley Owen realised that that sort of thing was not permissible, the better. He wasn't going to be as lenient as some ship's doctors, turning their glances the other way. The favoured niece of the shipping line's Chairman would soon find that out.

All the same, he couldn't forget the expression on her face as she looked back at him up there on the shadowy deck. Even her embarrassment had been underlaid with happiness, somehow emphasizing his own solitary state.

CHAPTER FIVE

As far as work went, the voyage promised to be un-eventful.

"Some trips are like this," Walker told Lesley as he cleaned the surgery next morning. "Just routine stuff and a few regular passengers with stock complaints, and a few more who panic at the first pang of sea-sickness and think they're going to die. Other trips rush us off our feet, with more patients than we can cope with easily. Times like that, we're hardly ever off duty. Once we had three childbirths, two tonsils, an acute appendix and an emergency op. which kept the doc. three hours at the table and Sister at the bedside night and day. 'Tweren't easy, I can tell you. Sister's been saying long enough that we needed an extra hand, and she was right."

"Well, it's nice to be told that. I was beginning to doubt it."

"Why? 'Cos Doc. didn't make you welcome? I shouldn't let that worry you."

"I don't. What does worry me is being made to feel in the way."

Walker flashed an amiable grin.

"Wait until the weather changes, Nurse, and the passengers begin spraining their ankles trying to brave the elements on deck, or half the ship is prostrate and the stewardesses can't cope. *Then* you'll find out if you're not needed!"

Reassured, Lesley departed to keep her promise to

Patsy Davis. Arriving at her stateroom, however, the stewardess met Lesley with the news that the girl felt much better and had gone to sit up on deck.

Lesley decided it might be tactful to visit old Lady Travitt next. She found her sitting up in bed reading the ship's newspaper, a compact little journal printed and edited on board and delivered first thing every morning to every cabin.

The woman's dyed hair was swathed in tulle, tied in a large bow on top of her head, but the raddled old face had not yet received its careful mask of make-up. This seemed to leave her oddly defenceless, and not for the first time Lesley thought that there was something pathetic about her.

"Ha!" the old lady barked without any preliminary greeting. "So it's you again."

"It is," Lesley agreed equably. "I called to see how you were this morning."

"Nice of you to take the trouble, I must say. Sister only comes when summoned."

"Sister has had to work single-handed until this voyage."

"And has now delegated you to her most tiresome patients, I have no doubt."

"I wouldn't say that. She has responsibilities which I, as her assistant, can't fulfil."

"And I suppose *I* am only worth the attention of an assistant?"

Lesley realised that whatever she said would be misconstrued by this difficult old woman, so she answered nothing more than, "Well, if you don't need me, I'll get back to the surgery."

"But I do need you!" There was a hint of sudden anxiety in the voice, an unexpected pleading which

58

suggested that all she wanted was someone's company. "What's your name, girl?"

"Lesley Owen."

"H'm. Nice name. I like it."

"Thank you."

"And I suppose you hope I'm going to like you, too?"

"Naturally, if I am to look after you."

"I don't *need* looking after! What do you think I am, an invalid? There's nothing wrong with me. Well, precious little, anyway. Just the odd dose of insulin needed now and then, that's all. And I must admit you didn't make a bad job of it yesterday."

"Then why did you complain to the doctor?"

"So he told you, did he?"

"Sister and I walked into the surgery when he was speaking to you on the phone. Then I heard him telling Sister what you said, or snatches of it."

"And I suppose you want me to apologise?"

"Not to me. To the doctor."

The old lady's surprise was only exceeded by Lesley's own. She had resolved to forget that unfortunate incident, and had determined not to harbour any resentment over it. Sister had assured her that Elvira's bark was worse than her bite, and a nurse had to get used to difficult patients, and especially to complaints, so the wisest thing to do was to forget them the moment they were done with. Yet here she was, aware of an anxiety to have the thing put right with the very man she disliked more than anyone else. It didn't make sense.

"Well," snapped Elvira Travitt, "I won't apologise. Not yet, anyway. If, by the end of the voyage, you've proved yourself a better nurse than I expect – well – perhaps I'll think about it."

Lesley wanted to laugh. She tried to check it, and

59

failed. Her frank young face quirked with amusement and the old lady's eyes widened in surprise. Her astonishment that anyone should be amused by anything she said, was so patent that Lesley's laughter doubled. She stood beside the bed, shaking with mirth.

"And what's so funny?" Lady Travitt snapped.

"You – I'm sorry, but it's the truth! – "

"*I*, funny? In what way?"

"The way you insist on being angry, tilting at windmills all the time and pretending they're dragons!"

The wrinkled mouth curved unwillingly.

"You make me sound a bit of a dragon myself."

"You're not really, but you do try to be, now don't you?"

The old lady pushed back the bedclothes and thrust her thin feet out of bed. "Be off with you! I'm going to bath and dress. No, no, *no* – don't help me! I'm not senile!" She trailed towards the bathroom, saying over her shoulder, "What off-duty time do you have, Nurse? During the afternoon, I mean."

"Half an hour's break for tea, then I'm on again until dinner."

"Have tea with me, then. In the main lounge." From the bathroom door the grotesque figure looked back. "Maybe I'll even like you when I get to know you better." With a sudden cackle she added, "Maybe *you* will even like *me*!"

I believe I like you already, Lesley thought to herself as she left the room. Having tea with Elvira Travitt might be amusing, and held the additional possibility of a further glimpse of Colin, who had been prevented from arranging their next meeting by the untimely advent of Mike Halliday last night. That was another reason for resenting the doctor.

She decided to return to Sick Bay via the main deck

and, on the way, to look out for Patsy Davis. Rows of luxury reclining chairs lined the long stretch, and amongst them moved stewards, handing round cups of beef tea, the normal shipboard elevenses. It took Lesley a little time to discover Patsy, whose deck chair had been placed in the lee of the port side.

There was colour in her cheeks and her eyes were bright.

"I feel wonderful, thanks to you, Nurse!" She smiled up at Lesley, indicating the foot of her chair. "Sit down and talk to me. I don't know a soul on board and besides, I like you."

There was refreshing candour about this girl.

"Does sea-sickness always leave a person feeling so wonderful?" she went on. "If so, I do believe it's worth going through!"

"I expect the wonder is finding one's self whole again."

"You're right. I felt as if my inside just didn't belong to me."

"And yet the sea wasn't very choppy. Are you normally a bad sailor?"

There was the briefest hesitation before Patsy answered, "Not normally, no."

A shadow fell across Lesley's lap and, looking up, she saw Colin smiling down on them. His fair head shone in the sunlight and, as always, his incredible good looks stirred her. She hoped her reaction didn't show.

"Good morning, Nurse." His smile was teasing.

"Good morning, Mr. Butler. Walking your morning mile round the deck?"

"I'm just finishing it – right here."

Because *you* are here, the words implied, but his eyes went beyond her to Patsy. Lesley introduced them and the girl smiled up at him, revealing even white teeth and an attractive curve of the mouth. She was so pretty that Lesley couldn't blame Colin for looking at her a little longer than was strictly necessary. Did he retain her hand a little longer than necessary, too?

They chatted for a while, Colin making no attempt to move on. "I must choose a deck chair," he said, his eyes observing the vacant place beside Patsy. "There's no name on that one – is it taken, do you know? If not, it's nicely sheltered here . . ."

"That's why I chose this spot," she answered.

"Would you mind if I shared it?"

"Of course not."

Colin summoned the deck steward, who inserted his name in the slot on the adjoining chair, then he stretched his well-tailored figure (even in casual wear Colin looked like something straight out of a male fashion journal) and smiled at both girls with his customary ease and charm.

"And how do you two come to know each other? You didn't tell me you had a friend on board, Lesley."

"I hadn't, except you."

How ridiculous, she thought, to class him as a mere friend!

Patsy Davis laughed.

"Nor had I, until Nurse came to me as a ministering angel last night and just about saved my life."

"You poor child." Colin's sympathetic glance focused on her. "The best cure for sea-sickness is champagne, did you know? You must have some with your lunch, and I will choose it for you. What is the number of your table? I'll have it sent over."

"I haven't booked my table yet. I was too ill to dine last night and had breakfast in bed this morning."

"Then I shall see that we have a table together. She obviously needs looking after, doesn't she, Nurse?"

Lesley smiled a little bleakly. It didn't mean anything, of course, but to address her professionally seemed a little chilling.

"I must get back to the surgery," she said. "I'm glad you're feeling better, Miss Davis."

"Patsy, please. Everyone calls me Patsy."

"Me, too?" Colin asked.

Lesley rose. She looked attractive in her white uniform, but compared with Patsy she felt ill-dressed. There was a wide gulf between herself and this passenger — the gulf of money.

She said good-bye and went on her way, wondering why a sudden lump had come into her throat. The morning had started well. She had wakened with a light heart, aware that all had come right between herself and Colin and that being on this ship, so close to him, was the most wonderful thing that could have happened. Even Lady Travitt's asperity had left her unperturbed, and the thought of Doctor Halliday mattered little. Yet now, after meeting Colin again, her optimism seemed to have diminished — which was illogical, of course, since his smile had held the usual quality of intimacy for her, and only last night she had been in his arms . . .

She thought in surprise, I'm jealous, that's the truth of it. Just plain jealous because those two are sitting side by side on deck and will do so every day. I'm jealous because Patsy Davis will see more of Colin than I shall; because they are fellow passengers and I am merely one of the crew.

She pulled herself together. Patsy was a nice girl and Colin was absolutely trustworthy, she was sure of that. It didn't matter to him that his fiancée was merely the ship's nurse, or that another girl was beautifully dressed and obviously moneyed. That glance of his, which had seemed to take in every detail of Patsy's appearance, had

certainly held no hint of calculation. The idea existed
merely in her own frightened heart.

But why the fear?

Sister was amused and pleased when she heard that
Lesley was to have tea with Elvira in the passengers'
lounge.

"Didn't I say she'd come round? She must like you,
my dear, or you wouldn't be so honoured."

"I think she is lonely and wants someone's company."

"She's lonely, all right, but if I know her, she wouldn't
share her precious tea time with someone uncongenial.
She would prefer to put the time to better use, such as
summing up her fellow passengers. Wait until you've
watched her scrutiny of them and heard her comments
about them! Shipboard gossip is meat and drink to her,
and if there isn't any, she'll start some. She can think up
more about her fellow travellers over one cup of tea than
I could on the entire voyage. You'll find her vastly enter-
taining and she will feed your unwilling ears with the
wildest speculations."

"Well, at least I am forewarned!"

The old lady's appearance at tea was certainly startling. She was as garish as a parrot, her dyed red hair
clashing with an emerald green and purple dress. But at
any rate she was an arresting figure, and the attention
she won obviously pleased her.

To Lesley's surprise, she chose a secluded table, but
the reason for this was soon evident – it commanded an
unrestricted view of the spacious lounge, and of everyone
in it.

Lesley, who had been on her feet all day, sank into
an armchair with a sigh of relief. The tea was nectar
compared with Walker's strong and bitter brew.

It was impossible to prevent her thoughts from winging

back to that other voyage, the voyage on which she had met Colin aboard the *Monarch*, for every afternoon they had lingered over tea in a lounge which might have been sister to this one. It had been a precious interlude whilst her father snoozed on deck, and it had been on just such an afternoon as this that Colin had looked at her across the low table and said, "Lesley, I'm in love with you. I know we've only just met and that all the sceptics would declare it impossible, but it hasn't taken me three days to realise that I want to marry you."

Just like that, he had said it, his compelling eyes pleading with her and his glance a caress. "Let's find a secluded spot," he had begged. "A corner on deck where no one can disturb us. I want to kiss you. Urgently."

It had been a wonder and an enchantment and a dream – but, unlike a dream, it had lasted. Colin's love had dominated her life from that moment.

"And if you ask *me*," old Lady Travitt was saying caustically, "he's not going to let the grass grow under his feet."

Lesley jerked to attention, realising she hadn't heard a word the old lady had said. But it didn't matter, for the dry voice continued, "Of course, he's an astute young man and he is never likely to miss an opportunity. I've seen his type aboard before."

So she had started already, had she – speculating about the passengers, just as Sister Collard had warned her. "What she can't find out, she will make up," Sister had said, adding that one had to humour this irascible but oddly likeable patient, which meant that while turning an attentive ear and making suitable noises of agreement, one could dismiss all she said. So Lesley was ready to let it all sail in one ear and out the other, and this, it seemed, was all the attention Elvira required, for she continued happily: "One day, of course, he'll meet his Waterloo. He certainly deserves to! I only hope that attractive young woman sees through him, but from the starry look in her eyes, I doubt it."

"More tea?" Lesley asked, taking Elvira's cup and refilling it. Glancing at her watch, she realised that in only five minutes she had to return to duty. She felt refreshed and ready for it. This brief half hour had been pleasant, with Lady Travitt unexpectedly amiable and her fund of gossip insufficiently accumulated to be disturbing. By the end of the voyage it might be a different matter.

Lesley handed the cup back with a smile. "I imagine there are always plenty of shipboard flirtations. People have so little to do, floating in idleness across the ocean. By the time we enter New York harbour all their trivial *affaires* will be petering out, and by the time we berth they will be finished altogether."

"I imagine that depends on whether his hopes are fulfilled or not – and, of course, on how far she is going on this trip."

"Whose hopes?" Lesley asked idly, remembering Sister's injunction to humour the old lady.

"Why, that handsome young man at the table in the far corner! Surely you know who I'm talking about? Or haven't you been listening properly?"

Lesley protested that of course she had been listening, and let her glance swerve across the room. Then it halted abruptly. Colin sat there, side by side upon a couch with Patsy Davis. They were laughing together, with obvious enjoyment. He looked very eye-catching in pale blue denims, with a matching shirt open at the neck and a masculine silver chain at the base of his throat, and Patsy was as enchanting as ever in yellow skin-tight hipsters worn with a white silk blouse tied carelessly round a bare midriff. The colour was back in her cheeks; she looked radiant.

A chill touched Lesley's heart. Of course, Colin was only being polite and amiable; hadn't he warned her that this was part of his job? But even his everyday, social smile could be devastating to a responsive heart. Not that he was aware of it. He was probably equally unaware that Patsy was spellbound, just as he was unaware that Lesley herself was watching and this astute old woman making the wildest and most ridiculous speculations about him.

"Handsome young devil, eh?" Elvira rapped.

Lesley admitted that he was very good looking.

"Rather more than that. *I*'d say he has an eye to the main chance and knows how to make the most of his looks *and* his opportunities."

Checking a sharp retort, Lesley merely asked, "What opportunities?"

"Use your eyes, girl! He's got that pretty little thing eating out of his hand already. Can't you see?"

"All I see is a man being courteous to a fellow traveller."

There was a chilly note to Lesley's voice which the old lady swept aside.

"Then you must be blind! Or are you deliberately making excuses for him? Why, for goodness' sake? What does it matter to you if an ambitious young man pursues the rich passengers?"

"I'm quite sure he does nothing of the sort!" Lesley found it impossible to keep indignation out of her voice. "You are being unfair, making wild guesses!"

"You think so, eh?" For a moment the shrewd eyes were speculative, then the bizarre shoulders shrugged, the glance lost interest. "Well, we shall see what we shall see."

67

We certainly will, thought Lesley with an inner smile. She could picture Elvira's surprise when learning – as she would eventually – that the handsome passenger was engaged to the ship's nurse. Meanwhile, if Patsy Davis had fallen under his spell, it was unfortunate but would only be temporary. Even so, Lesley felt sorry for the girl – which was illogical, since there was so much for which she could be envied.

"See the way he is looking at her!" the old lady went on (why *couldn't* she stop?). "That 'you're-the-only-woman-in-the-world' look only comes with practice, believe me."

"I *don't* believe you," Lesley retorted, forgetting Sister's instructions to humour the old woman. "You are guessing, that's all, and guessing wrongly."

The wrinkled mouth tightened, the eyes flared indignantly.

"Am I, indeed? And how do you know that, pray?"

"Because I happen to know Mr. Butler. What is more, I know him well. And now, if you will excuse me, I must get back on duty . . ."

She was gone before Elvira had a chance to answer, sparing neither the old lady, nor Colin, further attention. She didn't want him to think that she was spying on him, especially when there was no real cause for doubt or suspicion. So she missed his startled glance as she swept by.

But Elvira Travitt missed nothing. A gleam of interest came into her eyes. So I guess wrongly, do I, Nurse Owen? I don't think so, my girl! If anyone is wrong about that handsome young devil, it is you. And I'll prove it, what's more. I'll prove it before we get to New York, see if I don't!

CHAPTER SIX

THE telephone rang when Lesley was alone in the surgery. This was fortunate, because it was Colin's voice that echoed down the line.

"Darling, I want to see you – "

He detected a slight hesitation before she answered, "I'm busy, Colin."

"Not too busy to talk to me, I hope? Or is that lynx-eyed doctor around?"

"No. He's visiting Isolation."

"Then why can't we chat for awhile?"

"I'm on duty."

"Meet me when you come off."

He refused to heed the guarded note in her voice because he could overcome that if he had only five minutes alone with her. Perhaps she had been jealous this afternoon, but how was he to know that she'd be having tea in the main lounge? In any case, why shouldn't he be having tea there himself, and what did it matter if he shared it with another girl? Better in public than in private, and if Lesley raised any objection he would point that out to her.

He was anxious to restore himself in her favour because only this morning the ship's newspaper had featured an interesting item about the Chairman of the Line. Barnet Owen had achieved control of another industrial concern, and a big one. The thought that he had perhaps been too hasty in breaking his engagement to the man's niece reasserted itself in Colin's mind. She was still the man's god-daughter as well as his only niece, and there was still the flat in Belgravia which, after all, the man *had* offered to her . . .

But why the devil hadn't she told him that in the first place, Colin thought resentfully, instead of trotting out that line about a man's pride? No man who wanted to get on in the world would let pride stand in his way these days.

Colin's mood was one of mixed truculence and penitence. Perhaps Lesley was annoyed because he had left her so abruptly on the boat deck last night, and that was why she had swept by him in the lounge this afternoon, but surely she must realise that a speedy departure had been the wisest move on his part. He could have achieved no good with that intimidating doctor had he stayed, but women were funny creatures and Lesley might have expected his support. Colin resolved to make her see his point of view at the earliest opportunity. He had always found that singularly easy to do.

Meanwhile, he recalled the set expression on her face as she walked past himself and Patsy this afternoon. No doubt she had seen him, and been jealous. One of the ironies of breaking a relationship with a woman was that she invariably remained possessive. Women could never take no for an answer. He recalled, a trifle guiltily, that he had confirmed last night that he still wanted to marry her, but naturally he had not added the proviso that the whole thing depended on whether things went as he hoped. In a way, he supposed, she could be forgiven for assuming that their engagement had been reinstated, though from his private point of view he considered he had achieved the conveniently neutral position of being able to go in either direction, if he so wished.

Even so, Lesley needed careful handling. She was an emotional creature, so it would be tactful to appease her as soon as possible. A man had to play his cards right.

With little further persuasion, she agreed to meet him. The mere fact that he had telephoned, lulled her uneasiness. She told herself that her reaction to his having tea with Patsy had been silly, but now she realised that the thing which most disturbed her was not the fact that he had sought Patsy's company, but that he had so obviously been enjoying it.

She was aware that since the reversal in her affairs a sense of insecurity had grown within her, due mainly to Colin's behaviour. Despite his assurances, doubt had stirred. Could a man who really loved a girl bring himself to give her up?

But his delight in seeing her on board the *Regina* had been very evident and his kisses last night had been passionate. Her optimism rose, and so did her resolution. She had taken this job in order to be near him and to prove that she wasn't afraid of working, so there was no sense in defeating her own ends – and there was no surer way of doing that than to antagonise him through jealousy.

There was a tinge of impatience in his voice as he said, "Don't be late, will you? Apparently I'll see precious little of you on this trip if I don't badger you."

The surgery door opened abruptly and Mike Halliday entered. Lesley glanced at him, then turned back to the phone, making no attempt to hide the identity of her caller.

"All right, Colin – seven-thirty, in the bar of the Observation Lounge."

She ignored the doctor as she replaced the receiver, so the quick frown between his brows passed unnoticed. She even hummed lightly as she went about her duties, aware that her heart felt lighter because she now had something

71

to look forward to; a meeting with Colin which he himself had sought.

"You sound very happy, Nurse. Another illicit
meeting, I take it?"

She spun round indignantly, only to find the doctor
so close beside her that she bumped against him. His
body was large and disturbingly strong. His hands
gripped her arms, compelling her to be still. She
couldn't have escaped had she wanted to, which, oddly
enough, she didn't. There was something tremendously
reassuring about his masculine solidity, something
protective which made her feel weak and vulnerable, and
although she was independent by nature she found herself enjoying this wholly feminine reaction. She wanted
to draw close to him . . . closer and closer, even though
his grey eyes blazed with anger. But there was something
more than anger there, something so potent that it
could only be taken for jealousy.

She protested weakly, "Let me go—"

"Not until you answer my question." He shook her,
and she was conscious not only of his domination but of
her instinctive yielding to it. "That man is dating you
again, isn't he?"

She flung at him, "And why not?"

"Because – because—"

To his own bewilderment, he could not utter the
words which leapt into his mind: *Because I could kill any
man who wanted you.* The answer shocked him into
silence, but his hold tightened, and he felt himself
drawing her slender body towards his own until his arms
were around her and he was holding her closely and
passionately. Her senses whirled, as in some unbelievable
dream from which she had no desire to waken. This
couldn't be happening, of course. She was imagining the
whole thing – the strength of his arms and the passion of

him and the incoherent way in which he was murmuring her name over and over again. *"Lesley . . . Lesley . . ."*

She closed her eyes, locked fast in his embrace, her face uplifted, her lips slightly parted, carried away on a wave of desire which left her bemused. Remotely, a voice whispered in her clouded consciousness, "This is wrong, *wrong*! It is Colin you love, Colin you want . . ." but she was incapable of heeding it because only this man and this moment existed.

The dream shattered violently as he thrust her aside. Her eyes jerked open and she saw his face twisted with anger, but she had no way of knowing that the anger was directed against himself because he had surrendered to an overpowering force which seemed to be forever drawing him towards this girl, and he had to fight it because she threatened the safe edifice of his world, the solitude into which he had retreated as a safeguard against being hurt. No woman was going to be allowed to do that. Not ever again.

"Get away from me!" he flung at her. "Get back to your illicit meetings and your husband-hunting! Don't imagine *I* am going to fall for you too!"

Colin spent the next few hours at the Shore Excursion office on the Purser's deck, taking bookings for trips and suggesting others to passengers who didn't seem to know just what they wanted to do or see, and providing information about future ports of call. He was excellent at his job, had everything at his fingertips, and enjoyed nothing so much as meeting the ship's passengers, especially the rich ones. These were easy to weed out because he never had any difficulty in persuading them to take the most expensive excursions by private cars, which he booked on secret commission.

His looks and his charm won everyone over. "Madam,

I am here solely to help you; please call on me at any time! You want to visit the highlights of New York, the best shops, but you don't want to go with a group, by coach? Then I can plan a private tour for you and have it all mapped out by the time we dock, *and* a taxi waiting for you. And if you see any place *en route* during this cruise, which you would like to visit again next year, I'll be happy to arrange a holiday for you. And you, sir — book through Baynards and you can't go wrong! When we reach Jamaica I will personally show you the Blue Lagoon and Dragon Cove. Perhaps you'd like to go with a group by minibus, or in private cars? See either of these places, and you'll be eager to fix up next year's holiday on the spot . . ."

He was brisk, efficient, confident, suave, smiling and unendingly successful. At the end of the session he had reason to feel pleased with himself, and went in search of Patsy, who had promised to join him for a game of deck tennis. He was gratified because she was already waiting for him, but not so gratified when he saw her surrounded by three admiring men.

She looked very enticing in a pair of well-cut Bermuda shorts. Her figure was perfect, her legs long and shapely, her waist small and her hips narrow. She was one of the best looking girls he had ever met — but who *was* she? She didn't talk much about herself, although she was a lively conversationalist. By the time they had finished tea this afternoon he realised that she had learned a great deal about him, but yielded no personal information whatsoever. She was friendly, but reserved — a combination which he found tantalising.

His natural optimism re-asserted itself. He would soon learn all there was to learn about Patsy Davis and, meanwhile, he had the undeniable evidence of her financial state to reassure him. Money was advertised by her clothes, her expensive suite, and her air of luxury. She was so accustomed to it that it didn't occur to her to explain its source or to refer, even casually, to her parents' social standing – what other explanation was there for her reticence?

He waved to her and was gratified when she broke away from the cluster of admirers and came to meet him, eyes alight and a smile of sheer pleasure on her lovely face. He decided complacently that he had nothing to worry about. Patsy was going to be a great deal easier to handle than Lesley, and if all continued to go well in this new area he could shed the worry of Lesley once and for all. He would do it in a kindly way, of course, but a great deal more firmly than last time because he had a hunch that he was on a far more lucrative wicket with Patsy Davis.

And Colin's hunches were never wrong.

Lesley was careful to change out of her uniform before going to meet Colin this time, even though it meant being late. Perhaps it wasn't wise to appear too eager, anyway. She realised that she had always been the one to turn up first for any meeting.

"You might look in on Lady Travitt during the course of the evening," Maude Collard said as she went off duty. "Just pop in and see if she wants anything. That will keep her happy."

So Lesley went out of her way to call on the old lady. To her surprise, Elvira had already gone to bed. She was propped up, dining with a hearty appetite, her bed littered with discarded newspapers.

"Back numbers," she explained, jabbing at them with a fork. "Brought 'em with me. Had to. The ship's newspaper never prints any scandal. Dull, I call it."

Her bird-like eyes raked Lesley with an approving

glance. "H'm. You're looking very smart. Who have you dressed yourself up for?"

Lesley answered with what dignity she could muster, "I have merely changed out of my uniform, Lady Travitt," at which the old lady cackled.

"I can see that, stupid! But you're looking extra-specially nice. You've taken some pains with your hair and your make-up and at a guess I'd say you'd spent quite a time deciding what to wear."

"I haven't an extensive wardrobe to choose from." This was true. She had sold most of her model gowns to an exclusive wardrobe dealer in Mayfair before finally turning her back on the old life, for she knew that she would now have few opportunities to wear them.

Elvira snorted. "When I was young I could spend a couple of hours choosing between only two dresses! Did you?" she finished abruptly.

This had gone far enough, Lesley decided. The woman had an uncanny knack of going straight to the core of things, an ability to touch upon the truth.

"I came to see if you wanted anything, Lady Travitt."

Automatically, Lesley began to tidy the bed, sorting the litter of newspapers into a neat pile, but when she reached for one tucked beneath the bed-table the old lady's clawlike hand snatched it back.

"Leave that alone! Who told you to busy yourself with my things?"

Lesley checked a smile. So Elvira was in a mood, was she? Truculent and abusive. Already Lesley knew what to expect from this unpredictable woman.

She murmured an automatic apology, and put the pile of newspapers within reach again. "If there's nothing you want, I'll be on my way."

"And who said there wasn't? As it happens, there is. I want Doctor Halliday. Immediately."

"But he isn't on duty."

"I don't care about that. I want him. Fetch him, d'you hear?"

"Well, I'll try—" Lesley began doubtfully, but Elvira Travitt cut right across her words.

"Tell him *I* said he's to come. At once. It's important. Tell him that, too."

For the first time, Lesley observed a gleam in the old lady's eye which was more than her usual one of militant determination. There was an underlying excitement about it. "Go on, go on!" she commanded. "Quickly!"

"Why don't you telephone him?"

"Good gracious, Nurse, d'you think I haven't tried? He isn't in his quarters and he isn't in his surgery. So go ahead and find him. He'll come all right, if you say *I* sent you – though not quite so quickly as he would have done once upon a time, when my daughter Carol was travelling with me . . ."

The voice trailed away, suddenly tired. Even a little sad, Lesley thought.

She had difficulty in tracing the doctor and it was Walker who finally put her on his track. "He'll be in the gym, Nurse. He usually puts in an hour there before dinner. His way of keeping fit."

Walker was right. Mike was punching a medicine ball with a strength and accuracy that would have done credit to a professional boxer. Unobserved, she stood watching him for awhile. The muscles of his shoulders and back were impressive.

He stopped when he saw her, steadying the medicine ball with one gloved fist.

This was their first encounter since that incredible moment in the surgery, the moment which she insisted to herself had never happened because it was too fantastic to be true, but the sight of that athletic body of his

77

brought it all rushing back, and with it came self-consciousness and an almost unbearable shyness. She had to force herself to meet his eyes, and when she did, she was conscious of intense disappointment because they were cold and indifferent, which told her that any memory of that passionate contact between them lingered only in her own mind. It had meant so little to him that he had dismissed it, forgotten it.

Well, perhaps that was a good thing, even though it suggested that he considered her a girl to be picked up and dropped at will. Perhaps he could hardly be blamed for that, since he had seen her in another man's arms, in a secret rendezvous on the boat deck, the very first night at sea. The thought humiliated her.

She forced herself to say coolly, "Lady Travitt sent me to find you, Doctor. She wants to see you urgently. She says it's important."

To her surprise, a smile touched his lips.

"It always is!"

He held out his wrists to a gym attendant, who untied his gloves, peeled off the bindings beneath, and handed him a towel. Mike took it, saying over his shoulder: "Tell her I'll be along as soon as I've showered."

He spared Lesley no further glance and she departed with his message. She hurried because the incident had delayed her and she didn't want to arrive in the Obervation Lounge so late that she and Colin had no time to talk.

He was waiting, but not patiently. A slight frown creased his forehead but his smile was welcoming. He drew her onto a tall stool beside him.

"Darling, you're late," he reproached.

To his surprise, Lesley didn't apologise, merely saying that she couldn't get here earlier – and that was that. There was a sort of detachment about her, a suggestion of preoccupation that puzzled him. Had he but known it, it puzzled her too. To her own surprise, she was remembering not only that moment in the surgery, but Elvira's remark about the doctor and her daughter – and wondering what it implied.

Mike didn't obey the old lady's summons until he had changed and was ready to go down to dinner.

"You certainly didn't hurry," she rasped. "Or did that new nurse forget to mention that I wanted to see you immediately?"

"You do her an injustice, Elvira. She told me it was urgent."

The woman sniffed.

"A fact you seem to have ignored!"

"I came as soon as I was ready. I'm on my way to the dining room now. What do you want to see me about?"

Lady Travitt looked at him sadly. "Once upon a time, Mike, you would have come running. When Carol was with me, I mean."

His impassive face became, if possible, even more so. He waited, saying nothing, until she sighed and continued, "By the way, have you heard that she's getting a divorce?"

He was very still, revealing no reaction at all. The shock he felt, the wild leaping of hope and bitterness, were skilfully concealed.

"Is that what you wanted to tell me?"

"No. If you hadn't read of it before sailing, I knew you would hear the moment we arrived in New York. No," she repeated briskly, "I sent for you to show you something. This!"

Before offering the folded newspaper, the old lady glanced towards the door. "It is properly shut, I hope? Good. Well, look at *this*!"

Mike took the paper. The photograph of an extremely pretty girl looked back at him. The paper was slightly the worse for wear, but the features were unimpaired.

Lady Travitt's voice continued eagerly, "You can't think how glad I am that I brought these back numbers with me! Life was so rushed before sailing that I scarcely had time to even glance at the papers, so I bundled them all together to read on board. Wasn't it lucky?"

"Lucky? Why?" Mike's bewilderment was reflected in his voice.

"Good heavens, you recognise her, don't you?"

"Not in the least."

"Rubbish! She's next door!"

"In the next stateroom, you mean? I haven't visited it, I'm afraid."

"Well, you must have *seen* her! Everyone's seen her! She's the prettiest and best-dressed girl aboard this ship, and no wonder! Read what it says about her. Read it aloud, I want to hear it again. I've never been so excited!"

He obeyed.

"*Miss Patsy Davis, unanimously elected Miss E.E.C., was the only competitor actually holding the vital statistics laid down by the panel of experts in the first contest ever held to find the most beautiful girl from all member countries in the European Economic Community . . .*" He broke off with a grimace. "What on earth do you want me to read all this for?"

The bony hand waved impatiently.

"Go on, go *on!*"

"*Apart from her perfect measurements, Patsy was also judged the prettiest entrant and fully deserves her prize of £5,000 and a crown to commemorate her victory. When asked what she planned to do with the money, she answered gaily, 'Blue the lot of it, of course! Every penny! I've lived in a bed-sitter in Dulwich ever since I came to London to earn my living and*" *after four years of that all I want is a slice of luxury life and all that goes with it!'* ''

Mike raised his eyebrows in patient enquiry and was astonished by Elvira's ill-concealed excitement.

"There's more," she commanded. "Read it!"

" '*I suppose, if I had any sense, I'd save the money,*' Patsy continued, '*but that wouldn't get me out of my bed-sitter even for a month, would it? No, sir! I'm going to enjoy myself for the first time in my life, in the way I've always dreamed of. I'm going to sail across the Atlantic, see New York, and sail back again, and I'm going to do it in style. The most expensive suite, money in my pocket, and gorgeous clothes — that's every girl's dream, and why shouldn't I have it?*' When asked what she would do with the crown, which is made of silver inset with semi-precious gems, she laughed and replied, '*Leave it at home to flog, if necessary, when I come back — because I may not have a penny left and I'll have to give up my job to make this dream come true.*' And what is Patsy's job? '*I'm a typist, and not a very good one . . .*' ''

"And that's all," Mike finished, "except some facetious comment by the reporter about wishing her luck and finding a rich husband in the process." He threw the paper back on the bed. "What's it all about, Elvira? Why show it to me? If the girl's on board, good luck to her."

Elvira sniffed.

"Good luck is what she's going to need."

"Why?"

"Because *she* is the one that handsome young devil is after. The man our pretty nurse is in love with. Oh, yes, she is – don't look at me in that startled fashion. You may not be aware that Nurse Owen is head over ears in love with a handsome young schemer who obviously knows his way around, but *I* know it. What's more, it's my guess that she took this job to be near him. She knew him already, you see – I've found that out."

She was satisfied because, at last, she had won the doctor's interest.

"You know the man I'm talking about, Mike?"

"Yes, I believe I do. But what makes you think Nurse Owen knew him before coming aboard?"

"By the way she leapt to his defence when I spoke my mind about him. We were having tea together this afternoon and there he was, sitting close beside this Patsy-girl and lavishing all his attention on her, but when I said what I thought of him – *and* I wasn't wrong, mark you – that nurse of yours was highly indignant. 'He isn't like that at all!' she declared. 'I happen to know Mr. Butler. What is more, I know him well. . .' Oh, dear me, no, I mustn't utter a word of criticism against him."

"That doesn't mean there was anything between them before we sailed, or even that they had met."

"Since we sailed only yesterday afternoon, my dear boy, would that give her time to 'know him well'? Besides, I have an instinct for these things. That nurse of yours came on this ship in order to be near that man, and don't contradict me."

Mike was quiet a moment, then he asked, "Why are you telling me all this? Why did you want me to know about – that?" He indicated the discarded newspaper.

"Lot's of reasons! Because it's interesting, amusing, and exciting – and because it is fun to speculate on how the young man wille behav when he finds out."

"Perhaps he already knows."

"I doubt it. No – I think this plucky little Patsy Davis is going to keep quiet about the whole thing, if she can get away with it. That, to her, will be part of the dream – to actually live the part, to be accepted as a rich young woman travelling in a manner to which she is apparently accustomed. But the girl isn't a fool – oh dear me, no. Life hasn't been easy for her, and shrewdness is learned in a hard school – or a cheap bed-sitter. Mark my words, no one knows her story. Least of all Colin Butler – yes, that's his name, I've found that out too – and that attractive nurse of yours."

"And why should it concern Nurse Owen?"

"Patsy's private affairs don't, but Butler's attentions to her most certainly do. I've *told* you, Mike, she's in love with the man."

Inexplicably, Mike was troubled, but he was also annoyed. So Lesley Owen had wangled a job aboard the *Regina* in order to be near the man she loved, had she? Not because she was interested in nursing or cared about the job, merely so that she could carry on a love affair. All things considered, the situation was worse than before. The thought that this spoilt young niece of the company's Chairman had been able to land such a job for such paltry reasons angered him thoroughly.

He turned away. "That matter is of no interest to me, Elvira."

The bird-like eyes darted after him.

"Then it should be."

"And why?"

"Because you're not going to get the best work out of your nurse if her heart is broken."

"And why should it be?"

"Why indeed, when you and I can prevent it?"

"And how?" He was half amused, half irritated, but the compassion he always felt for the old lady made him listen to her.

"By letting her find out for herself that the man she loves simply isn't worth loving. That way, at least, her pride will be preserved. The worst thing that could happen would be for her to learn the truth from some-one else." A conspiratorial note crept into Elvira's voice. "Whatever we do, we mustn't tell her, or *any*one, the truth about Patsy Davis. Let that girl keep her secret for as long as she wishes – Colin Butler is sure to find out in the end, and *then* Nurse Owen will see him in his true colours."

Mike shrugged.

"To tell you the truth, it matters little to me whether she does or not."

Lady Travitt made no answer, but her wrinkled mouth smiled wryly. My dear Mike, she thought, you're lying!

She felt a sudden quickening of interest. On top of everything – the fun of this discovery and the interest of watching those three young people – there was now *this*; this thing which Mike, with characteristic stubbornness, was apparently determined not to acknowledge. Perhaps he couldn't even see it. But she could. Yes, indeed, she could see it very clearly. She saw a lot and she saw it well, and it all gave her supreme satisfaction. To fall in love with someone else, to forget Carol completely, would be Mike Halliday's salvation.

The old lady said briskly, "But you admit that the girl's work is important, don't you? You admit that you want your nurse to give of her best? Very well, then, be guided by me and help me to cure her! We must keep quiet about Patsy Davis. Let this handsome young schemer go on believing her to be rich, and both his eyes and Nurse Owen's will be opened in time."

"And what about warning poor little Patsy?"

"Poor little Patsy is more capable of taking care of herself than your highly competent nurse when it comes to affairs of the heart. It wouldn't surprise me if Patsy saw right through him."

An unwilling smile touched Mike's lips.

"So Nurse Owen is 'highly competent' now, is she? Last night you complained that she was the reverse."

Elvira ruffled like an indignant old hen.

"Be off with you! But not before you promise – you know what."

"All right," he agreed reluctantly. "I promise."

CHAPTER SEVEN

"Look, darling," Colin said uneasily, "about this afternoon—"

"What about this afternoon?" Lesley echoed.

"Did you really mind my having tea with Patsy? You looked as if you did. That was why you pretended not to see us when you hurried out, wasn't it?"

This was so completely true that Lesley couldn't deny it. "I was silly," she admitted. "Forget it, please."

"You were," he agreed. "Our being together didn't mean a thing, you know. She's a nice kid and since you're not available all the time, I must have *some*one's company."

"Colin, honestly, you don't have to explain or make excuses."

"I'm not making excuses. I just want you to understand."

"I do."

He gave her arm a squeeze. His smile was warm and disturbing. She thought again, as she had thought a thousand times before, that Colin really was the most handsome man she had ever met. So it seemed illogical that a picture of Mike Halliday's strong features should be lingering in her mind.

Colin urged, "Drink up, my sweet, and let's enjoy ourselves. You're off for the evening, I hope?"

She agreed, very happily, that she was.

"Then we'll get up a party and go on to the Verandah Grill at midnight. You'd like that?"

"I'd love it, but I'll have to change. This frock is too informal."

She was glad she had taken the precaution of packing an evening dress, though she had wondered at the time if she wasn't being over-optimistic. Her chances of dancing with Colin had seemed remote, but she had packed an uncrushable lace dress on the off-chance. Now she blessed her foresight.

"See you after dinner, then," said Colin.

She was surprised, on entering the dining room, to see Mike Halliday sitting at one of the tables reserved for ship's personnel. Last night he had dined in his own quarters – which, Sister Collard had told her, he preferred. Since the table was the one to which she had been allocated, Lesley walked across to it and, as she did so, Mike glanced up. He watched her approach with interest.

What was this? he thought cynically. A dress parade? She had not been wearing a full-length gown when she had sought him in the gym earlier this evening, but a little velvet affair in which she had looked very attractive. Now she looked elegant and, he admitted unwillingly, even rather beautiful. She had a certain poise which he would have admired in anyone else.

He rose politely and held her chair for her, but, as usual, she detected a certain irony in his courtesy. It was certainly in his voice as he said, "How magnificent you look, Nurse! I presume all this splendour is for the benefit of the ballroom later this evening? I'm glad that the medical staff is to be so well represented amongst the celebrities."

She ignored the sarcasm in his voice. Nothing, she realised, would give this man greater satisfaction than to know that his shafts went home, so she gave a cool little smile as she picked up the enormous menu.

87

The dining steward was gratified by her choice. Here was someone who really knew how to order – unlike the doctor, who seemed to care little about what was put before him. Give him a steak or a lamb chop and he'd be satisfied. Flights of culinary fancy were wasted on him.

Maude Collard, being still on duty, was in uniform. She looked a trifle enviously at Lesley and said, "My dear, what a lovely dress! It must have cost a fortune."

"Not exactly." Lesley smiled.

The doctor put in drily, "Have you forgotten, Sister, that Nurse Owen is no ordinary working girl?"

Lesley's eyes sparked. For a moment Mike thought she was about to make some stinging rejoinder, but she checked herself and answered smoothly, "I'm glad you like it, Sister. As a matter of fact, it is three years old and I made it myself."

"Then you're a very clever girl," Maude said sincerely.

"Not really. I enjoy dressmaking."

"As a sort of creative slumming?" Mike put in. "I suppose you regard it as something of a novelty."

Refusing to be provoked, Lesley continued talking to Sister. "It's a very simple dress, really. When I was nursing my father, I used to watch the dressmaking series on T.V. when he took his afternoon sleep, and the basic pattern I learned can be adapted in all sorts of materials."

They embarked upon a wholly feminine discussion of fashion, Lesley offering to help Maude with the making of a dress, if she wished. The older woman, who had struggled unsuccessfully more than once, accepted eagerly. It amused Maude to observe Mike's sceptical glance. It was plain that he refused to believe that the indulged niece of Barnet Owen could be a useful or competent young woman. But he'll learn, Maude thought serenely. He'll learn one day, poor man, and I hope I'm around when he does.

Mike finished his meal and left the two women discussing materials. "I'll get some tomorrow," Maude decided. "The shops on board carry good stocks, especially of tweeds and woollens, which the Americans go for in a big way. What do you suggest I buy? Lightweight wool, or tweed?"

"It depends on the style and when you want to wear it – " Lesley broke off as a vision drifted into view. It was Patsy Davis, making a spectacular entrance in a cloud of flame chiffon. "If Doctor Halliday really wants to see an expensive gown," she said, "he should take a look at *that*. Top couture and an exclusive model . . . "

Maude chuckled. "What a pity he's gone! What do you think it cost, my dear? You're a better judge than I. The nearest *I* ever get to model gowns is right here on the *Regina*, admiring them on other women. That must have cost the earth, don't you think?"

Lesley's eyes were filled with genuine admiration. "Whatever the cost, it was worth every penny. And how beautiful she looks in it! She really is one of the loveliest girls I've ever seen. Do you think she's an actress or a film star or something?"

"My dear, if she were anything in the theatrical line, the publicity boys would have announced her coming. No star, established or potential, sails on this ship without a fanfare in the press."

"Then she must be rich in her own right."

"So what? You're not envious, surely? Not *you*, Lesley. You can match her in looks any day. Well, you can hold a candle to her, at least. And now I must get back to Sick Bay. Enjoy yourself tonight, and make the most of it because it will be *your* duty turn tomorrow night." With a nod and a smile she departed, just as Patsy drifted past their table and, seeing Lesley, flashed her warm and friendly smile.

"Hello, Nurse – how nice you look. And dining alone – what a waste!"

Lesley laughed.

"I haven't been alone. I've had Sister and the doctor for company."

Patsy lingered. "The doctor looks nice, although I haven't met him yet. Not that I want to, as a patient! Still, there's something about doctors, isn't there? Something attractive; sort of challenging, I always think."

"Not about this one," Lesley said without thinking, then added hastily, "One gets a different impression, working with them."

Patsy looked surprised. "Yet a lot of nurses marry doctors, don't they?"

"I believe so."

A dimple flickered beside Patsy's mouth.

"Perhaps you'll finish up by marrying this one. He's a bachelor, I hear."

"And as far as I am concerned, he can remain one."

Oh dear, thought Patsy, I seem to have said the wrong thing. But I wonder why she dislikes the man – and couldn't that be significant? The attraction of opposites, perhaps, like Colin Butler and myself . . . The thought made her heart accelerate. We're not a bit alike, really, and I know it. But *he* doesn't – yet. And I know how he'll react if he ever finds out.

"Colin tells me you're joining our party tonight. I'm glad."

Patsy was incapable of pretence and her liking for the ship's nurse was genuine, but she could not understand Lesley's little start of surprise.

90

Our party? Lesley thought. Hers and Colin's?

She forced a smile and answered, "Yes. I am looking forward to it."

The dining steward hovered at Lesley's elbow again. She ordered *crêpe suzette* and Patsy moved on, saying over her shoulder, "See you later, then."

She drifted away, her cloud of chiffon clinging to her lovely figure. The dress was modelled on Grecian lines and her neck rose from it like the slender stalk of a flower, capped by the golden bloom of her head. She had spent a couple of hours with the hairdresser this afternoon, and the result was good. So it ought to be, she reflected wryly as she walked to a distant part of the restaurant where Colin waited at their table. That hairdo cost me as much as a week's wages at home – but golly, it was worth it! It will be something to remember when I'm doing it myself again.

Colin's eyes admired and reproached her.

"I thought you were never coming, and now you are here I never want to let you out of my sight." His glance appraised her gown and openly admired it.

She lowered her eyelashes in mock modesty and said, "I am glad you approve, sir."

"Approve! I'm not the only man doing that right now. Didn't you see the heads turning like a tidal wave as you went by?"

"How gratifying! Just the result I hoped for," she answered with a laugh, very nearly adding with a touch of irony that she had paid for it, too.

She took the gigantic menu which a swiftly attentive steward proffered, thanking her stars it was printed in English and therefore saved her the agony of pretending to understand French. When she had ordered, she sat back with a sigh of contentment, letting her glance slide appreciatively about the restaurant. Last night she had been too ill to dine. Now she felt wonderful and was prepared to enjoy herself.

She was eager to savour every moment. She had read the ship's guide book from cover to cover and knew that, apart from the Verandah Grill and three private dining rooms, this one seated six hundred people, and that the decorative wood sculptures on the walls were almost as valuable as the immense tapestries lining the main staircases. It was hard to suppress a sense of awe as she looked about her, wondering which of her fellow travellers laid claim to the royal titles featured on the passenger list. And here am *I*, she secretly marvelled, plain Patsy Davis from Dulwich, hob-nobbing with the rich – just as if I belonged!

"A penny for them," Colin said, a little peeved because she had forgotten him.

"They're worth much more!" Her widely-spaced eyes smiled into his, but he thought he detected a question in them, an uncertainty, as if she were on the brink of saying something and then thought better of it. The reappearance of the steward broke into the moment and Colin was left with the feeling that he had been defrauded of his first real moment of contact.

Patsy turned her attention to the *hors d'oeuvres,* thankful that she had resisted the temptation to confide in him. For one brief second she had been on the point of confessing that all this was new and thrilling to her, an experience she was never likely to have again. The ball would end for her as it had done for Cinderella, but there would be no fairy prince or golden coach to bring down the curtain. When it was all over it would be back to the bed-sit, for her. So she was glad she had not revealed the truth to Colin. She felt unsure of her ground with him. He attracted her, even disturbed her in a new and unfamiliar way, but instinct made her wary. She had not known him long enough for confidences and after they reached New York she might never see him again, for she left the ship there to spend two lavish weeks ashore, returning to Southampton at the end of them on *Regina's* sister ship, the *Monarch,* while Colin sailed on to far blue horizons, to places with romantic-sounding names, and more new acquaintances, new girls no doubt.

She had to remember that all this was a brief chapter in her life, no more. A chapter of adventure and glamour and luxury. It would be a pity to spoil it by revealing the truth.

Colin was smiling at her across the table, and now he leaned across and said softly, "Patsy, darling, you are lovely. But you know that, of course. You must have been told it a thousand times."

She thought with a spurt of inner amusement, better than that, I've been paid for it! She was honest enough to accept her good looks as bounty bestowed by a generous fate, but not without the reflection that it owed her something after all. Life had not been particularly generous to her in other ways. She had lost her parents in a coach crash when she was very small and had been brought up by foster parents who, though kind, could never really replace her true mother and father. Since growing up, she had had to stand on her own two feet. Of course, she had been crazy to blue her prize money on a trip like this – everyone had told her so – but she didn't regret it. It made up for all the stinted years behind her and, in an illogical way, helped her to face the future more optimistically. After all, she thought candidly, I'm young and healthy and can earn my living, and hard work never frightened me.

"Your thoughts are miles away." Colin reproached. "Come back from wherever you are, eat up that soufflé,

93

and then let's get along to the ballroom. There's dancing there until midnight, after which we'll go along to the Verandah Grill and dance until dawn."

After dinner they had coffee and liqueurs in one of the exotic garden lounges, heavy with the perfume of hot-house blooms, and in a mood of dream-like wonder Patsy descended to the ballroom at Colin's side. It was the most natural thing in the world to feel his arm linked in her own, and so complete was her sense of ease that she made no attempt to suppress her delight when they reached it. The walls were richly quilted in oyster satin, and looking aft was a large orchestra platform equipped with recessed lighting. The bays on each side of the room were lined with ivory sycamore and decorated with silver stars. The whole thing was like something from a film set – exotic and a little unreal. Patsy stood on the threshold and clasped her hands in wonder.

"I've never seen anything so beautiful in my life!"

Colin regarded her with amused indulgence.

"Sometimes, Patsy, you're as naïve as a child. I can't understand it, but I like it."

She pulled herself together, quickly.

"Have you never travelled on this line before?" he asked.

"Not on this particular vessel," she answered truth-fully and, going into his arms, felt herself swung onto the dance floor, rather as Cinderella must have felt at the ball.

They had danced three encores before Patsy saw Lesley sitting alone in a distant recess. Guilt smote her. "Oh, Colin, we forgot that nice nurse! How absolutely *awful* of us! We must make it up to her at once. Dance with her, Colin."

He had the grace to feel ashamed. He crossed guiltily to Lesley, seized her hand and said, "At last we've found you! Why are you hiding over here? We have a reserved table over on the port side – come along."

Before she could answer he was propelling her across the crowded room. At the edge of the dance floor he slipped his arm about her, saying easily, "We'll dance our way across. That will give me a chance to hold you ..."

Her face was very still, her eyes unrevealing, but he felt oddly disturbed.

"What's the matter, Lesley? You seem somehow – withdrawn."

"Do I?"

"Oh, come off it, Lesley!" He gave her a friendly shake. "Not jealous again, I hope? If there's anything I can't cope with, it's jealousy."

She took a deep breath. She knew it would be unwise to reveal her hurt, but it persisted nevertheless. For quite a time she had been watching him dance with Patsy, and not even she could delude herself that he had eyes for anyone but his partner. When they had entered the ballroom he had not even troubled to glance around, so it was useless to pretend that he had been looking for her.

The awful part of it was that it was all so familiar, like a movie being run off twice, but with the characters changed. Previously it had been she, Lesley Owen, who had been the focus of his attention; he had had eyes for no one else on that other memorable voyage. Now there seemed to be a pattern in his behaviour which she didn't want to acknowledge, but Elvira Travitt's words echoed unpleasantly in her ears: "*What does it matter to you if an ambitious man pursues the rich passengers?*"

But of course it wasn't pursuit. His job was to make contacts on behalf of his travel firm, to arrange trips ashore and to interest them in booking future holidays, so, naturally, he would go for those with money and Patsy, obviously, had plenty of that. And somehow she couldn't be jealous of Patsy as a person; she was too nice. So she smiled at Colin, effort though it was, and he gave her a companionable hug.

"That's my girl!"

My girl?

Her spirits lightened, especially when their party increased; a couple of American businessmen and their wives, a charming Austrian playwright, and a friendly English couple from the Midlands. By midnight the party was in high spirits and by the time they moved on to the Verandah Grill Lesley's heart was light and gay.

Only two incidents marred the evening. One occurred during the interval between the ballroom session and the later party, when she, Colin, Patsy and the Austrian went on deck for a breath of air. The Verandah Grill had not yet opened its doors to dancers and it was Colin who suggested a stroll outside meanwhile. Walking from the ballroom to the promenade deck took them past the surgery, and Lesley noticed a light within. Was Mike at his desk again, working? Sister had told her that he put in hours of writing when his duty was over, and last night, when she had gone to the dispensary to mix something for Patsy, he had obviously been hard at it.

The door opened at that precise moment, and the doctor emerged. He looked tired, she thought, and because he had not seen her she was able to study him briefly, struck by something she had not noticed before – an air of solitariness which seemed out of keeping with his self-sufficiency. She felt as if she were seeing him for the first time, and this time as he really was – a lonely man, even perhaps an unhappy one.

The idea was purely fanciful, and dispelled when he

looked at her. There was a touch of ironic amusement in his eyes which implied more than she cared to see. His eyes flickered to Colin. She was glad that he saw them together again because it proved that she cared nothing for his comments and that her private life was her own.

He greeted her politely and went on his way – a tall, rangy figure which Colin regarded with a sort of detached interest. "Isn't that the ship's doctor? Can't say I care much for the look of him."

"Why not?"

"Too grim by half. What makes him so stern? Bad temper, I suspect. I don't envy you, working for a man like that."

Illogically, she was defensive at once.

"He isn't grim, Colin. Just serious."

"Well, of course, if you *like* that type of man . . . "

"I didn't say I liked him. I just wanted to be fair to him."

She couldn't think why. He had not been fair to herself from the moment she came aboard, and even in a passing glance, such as he had bestowed on her just now, his antipathy was barely concealed. Even so, she felt sorry for him somehow. Quite unnecessarily, she knew, for a man like Mike Halliday neither needed nor wanted anyone's pity.

He disappeared just as Patsy and the Austrian caught up with them. For the most part Lesley had been paired off with the Austrian all evening, but she hoped that from now on things would change. And at that precise moment she felt Colin's arm fall away from her waist. She supposed it was natural, for they had reached the gates of the lift and now he reached forward to press the button for it.

But later, as she undressed for bed and thought drowsily

back over the evening, the other disturbing thing occurred to her – she had been paired off again with the Austrian from the moment they entered the Verandah Grill, and Colin had made no attempt to take her from him.

Mike gave Lesley a searching glance when she reported for duty next morning, and said at once, "I am aware that your private life is your own and that what you do during off-duty hours is no concern of mine, but the state in which you report for work *is* my concern. Therefore I am entitled to protest when you arrive with shadows under your eyes and obviously tired. In future, please make a point of being in bed at a reasonable hour."

What he said was absolutely true, so she had no answer. She *was* tired. Dancing until three o'clock in the morning was unwise when one had to be on duty again at eight. And she had slept badly when at last she had gone to bed, troubled by a constantly recurring picture of Patsy and Colin dancing together, smiling in an intimate, personal sort of way. If the girl wasn't in love with him already, she was half way there.

When embarking on this plan to show Colin that she was not averse to working, Lesley had not anticipated the advent of another girl. She had imagined only herself and Colin, reunited on board the *Regina*, seizing every spare moment alone together, with nothing but blue horizons ahead. It was perfectly natural to assume that two people in love would fall into each other's arms at the first opportunity – and so they had done, but only secretly.

To her surprise, the doctor threw her a sympathetic glance and finished more gently, "You'd better knock off early today and get a good night's sleep. We're not busy at the moment, but the weather forecast isn't too good and if seas get high we could be rushed off our feet."

He dismissed her with a nod and she went on her way to the Isolation Ward, where Sister Collard met her with news that the case of measles was now out of quarantine and the patient could be transferred to her own quarters. "You can get Doctor Halliday to sign the certificate, and the mumps should be signed off tomorrow, thank goodness – such a restless child, with his adoring Mum constantly flapping around and criticising everything we do." Sister sighed philosophically, and finished, "Did you have a good time last night? You certainly look as if you did!"

"I know – I look tired, Sister. Don't you scold me too."

"So the doctor's been at you, has he?"

"Not too harshly, and not unjustly. I did stay up late. I promise I won't again."

"That's all right, my dear. Momma Mumps will be only too pleased to keep Junior amused all day, and once Measles has been moved out, you'll be able to take things easy. Now I'm off to buy that dress material. The shop displaying Scottish goods has some super cashmere. We could cut it out on the surgery table this afternoon. How about it?"

"I'd enjoy that. What colour are you thinking of?"

"Something dark and slimming. Navy or black, I suppose, though I must say I do get sick of them."

"They have some nice stuff in a mixture of heather and wine. It would cut and hang beautifully and be just as slimming, I'm sure."

"I'll take a look at it."

Maude bustled away in happy anticipation. She was enjoying having this girl aboard. It was pleasant to have the companionship of someone of her own sex as a change from Mike's masculine reserve, and Lesley Owen had turned out to be completely different from expectations. She was sensible and thoroughly nice. She knew she would miss the girl very much if she left the *Regina*, and she feared that if Mike's attitude towards her didn't change it was more than likely that he would succeed in getting rid of her. He had a hell of determination, that man, a useful characteristic where his work was concerned but not always an asset in his personal relationships. He would work unflaggingly at anything he undertook; she only hoped he would not pursue his campaign against Lesley in the same way.

Sometimes Maude suspected that Mike harboured a resentment against all women; she herself had found him difficult to work with at first. His reserve was an armour which had taken some time to penetrate and she was well aware that she was the first Sister to survive more than one voyage with him. And yet she liked him, and respected him, and sometimes she glimpsed the real side of him when handling patients, for then the sincere, compassionate man emerged. What she could not understand was why he had to hide behind some sort of mental screen at other times.

Maude purchased the heather-coloured material (Lesley had been right about it – it was absolutely "her") and carried it back triumphantly to the surgery. As she expected, Lesley was there, going over supplies with Walker. Mike was at his desk in the consulting room, apparently lost in thought. He was usually intent on some task or other, but this was the first time Sister had ever seen him staring into space.

The sound of her step jerked him back to awareness.

"I thought you were off duty," he said.

"I am, but I couldn't wait to show this to Lesley." She indicated her parcel.

If he noticed the lack of formality in her reference to her junior, he ignored it. Mike was something of a traditionalist and Maude knew that the swift friendship which had mounted between herself and Lesley would not please him. In the beginning, she and the doctor had been united in opposition, but now she had gone over to the girl's side, which reduced the opposing ranks to one stubborn male, and how could one lone man hope to stand up against two women? The thought amused her. Fond as she was of the recalcitrant doctor, she would enjoy seeing him come to heel – especially the heel of a nice girl like Lesley.

After the door into the main part of the surgery had closed behind her, Mike sighed impatiently. What was the matter with him, that he could no longer concentrate? All morning he had been unable to settle to anything, attending to routine jobs with half his mind running on his conversation with Elvira. What was it to him if Nurse Owen had taken this job in order to be near the man she loved? He should be glad, for it could mean that she might marry and get out of his way, once and for all.

But even that idea didn't make any difference. Since their meeting in the corridor last night (Butler's arm had been about her waist, he remembered) he had been unable to forget how happy she had looked. She had reminded him of Carol when their passion for each other had been mutual and unrestrained . . .

The thought of Carol increased his restlessness. Elvira's news about her divorce had startled him although, in a way, he knew he shouldn't be surprised. He had always known that one day she would tire of her rich American husband, twenty years her senior and father of a grown-up family by the time she became his third, and youngest, wife. Tad Wilmott was one of New York's most famous impresarios, and his interest in Carol's talent had been genuine enough at first. And, of course, Carol had always been ambitious. Elvira herself had warned him about that.

"I know my daughter," she had said quite frankly. "From childhood, she got whatever she wanted, and she'll go on getting it. And, believe me, what she wants isn't life as a country doctor's wife, and I know that is what you really want to be. I've spoilt her, I'm afraid, and other people have been carrying on the good work. It would have been better for her if she hadn't been so beautiful, but no one can resist her."

That was true. He had been unable to resist her himself, and had stubbornly refused to believe her mother's predictions. He had even applied for this appointment so that he could see her in New York after she had got her first theatrical engagement there. It hadn't lasted long – like their love affair. After a short run, it was followed by Wilmott's wooing, which had been even shorter. Within a month, Carol became the third Mrs. Wilmott, while Mike remained an unknown doctor at sea, still in love with her and refusing, for a long time, to believe that she could place ambition above everything else.

"My dear boy," said Elvira, "Carol never loved anyone but herself. This marriage won't last. You'll see,"

He had not expected Elvira to be proved right, and so quickly. Less than two years! During that time Carol's mother had crossed the Atlantic regularly to see her, refusing to fly because she didn't trust airplanes. She never missed a production of her daughter's, and nor did he. But now she was a star in her own right and didn't even need Wilmott any more.

He had to face the truth. Even though bitterness had replaced his earlier feeling for Carol, he had always sought excuses for her, defended her, made allowances for the artistic temperament with which she was so liberally endowed. But he had been desperately hurt and avoided women ever since. The only one for whom he had any time was Maude Collard, middle-aged and loyal and hard-working. Young women weren't made like Maude nowadays. They were selfish and spoilt and not to be trusted.

Take this girl, Lesley Owen. She was after her own ends, pursuing the man she wanted. She wouldn't be aboard, otherwise. All she wanted was Colin Butler, who already had that poor little beauty queen eating out of his hand. Why did women fall for a man like that? Mike had seen it happen a hundred or more times. On every voyage there would be a man like Colin Butler, and few women ever found them out.

But as far as he was concerned, what did it matter? Lesley Owen could go right ahead and make a fool of herself, and Patsy Davis could weave her fancy dreams and break her foolish little heart. She was getting her money's worth, wasn't she? She was having her slice of luxury life with a good dollop of romance thrown in, so she couldn't grumble if, at the end of it, the fellow ditched her. Butler was much more likely to marry the niece of the company's Chairman, and it was extremely doubtful whether Lady Travitt's scheme to open Lesley's eyes would work. Mike had a shrewd idea that Colin Butler knew how to play his cards.

From beyond the dispensary door came the sound of feminine voices. Sister Collard and Nurse Owen certainly seemed to be getting along well together; the girl had won Maude over completely. That surprised him. It also left him bereft of an ally. Between them, they could have got rid of this unwelcome nurse. Now he would have to do the job single-handed.

The dispensary door opened and Sister emerged,

carrying her parcel, now unwrapped. He saw a roll of material and heard her say over her shoulder, "Till this afternoon then, Lesley. I'll come down around three o'clock." To Mike she said happily, "You won't be needing the surgery table, will you, Doctor? We want to use it."

"For a dressmaking session, I gather. Well, it will be the first time an operating table has ever been put to that particular use! Since we're not busy, I can hardly refuse."

"Why should you?" she answered serenely.

He retorted, "I hope this tiresome new nurse won't turn the place into a beauty parlour next."

"That, if I may say so, Doctor, was a very peevish remark. I'm surprised at you."

He smiled unwillingly.

"Well, it makes a man wonder. Sewing bees in the surgery could conceivably lead to other feminine activities."

"It's extremely kind of Lesley to help me," Maude answered severely. "There isn't a table big enough in either of our cabins, so why should you mind?"

"I note you're on Christian name terms with her already."

"Do you mind that, too? Lesley's a pretty name and she's too nice to stand on any formality with."

Maude nodded in her friendly way and departed to get some sleep.

The encounter increased his restlessness. He decided to go on deck for some air; a brisk walk might work off some of his ill humour. He chose the sports deck where three full-sized deck tennis courts afforded ample space, with vast areas on the port and starboard sides for promenading, clay pigeon shooting, shuffle-board and other activities. At the end was a wide balcony from which spectators could watch players on the squash court, and it was here that he saw Colin Butler teaching Patsy the rudiments of the game.

A voice beside him said drily, "What did I tell you? Wastes no time, does he? And it doesn't seem to occur to him that if that girl were the heiress he probably imagines, she would have had previous opportunities to play this game."

Elvira's sharp eyes darted to Mike with an air of conspiracy which he wanted to ignore. He had no desire to be drawn into the affairs of the passengers, and as far as he was concerned it mattered little what Colin Butler did, whom he pursued, or with what aim.

But he didn't underestimate the man's intelligence, as Lady Travitt appeared to. It seemed to him that Colin observed Patsy pretty closely, and not merely because she was pretty. The man was observant and, very possibly, shrewd. But his attentions to this girl seemed to be intensified when Lesley was not around.

Sidestepping the subject, Mike said, "To look at that sea, one would be tempted to ignore the weather forecast. So far, this has been one of the calmest crossings I've known."

"And does it threaten to break?"

"According to the radio, yes."

"How tiresome! That means half the passengers will be confined to their beds, including myself, and I will miss all the fun."

"There won't be any, if it gets really rough."

"Oh, I didn't mean dancing and gaiety, and you know it. Don't try to sidestep, Mike. I've done this crossing often enough to know what happens when bad weather gets up – all the shipboard flirtations fizzle out; the dining room is half empty and the decks deserted. A few people totter about, trying to pretend they are tough and looking singularly unattractive in varying shades of pea green. As for romance, it blows away on the wind. There's absolutely nothing to do then but pray for a sight of New York harbour and resign oneself to being delayed indefinitely." She sighed. "I'm a bad sailor, too. How tiresome of Carol to live on the wrong side of the Atlantic!"

"You know you enjoy these crossings, Elvira, bad weather or no."

"So long as I don't miss the shipboard goings-on – yes, I do. But I hate the thought of not seeing the outcome of *this* particular situation. It's interesting, don't you think? And you know perfectly well I'm referring to your nice nurse and her love affair."

The game of squash was over and Patsy, laughing and breathless, came climbing up, with Colin beside her. She looked radiant.

"Good morning, Miss Davis. You don't know me, but it's time we met. I am your next door neighbour, Elvira Travitt."

The old lady held out a clawlike hand, heavy with rings, and Patsy took it in a friendly grasp. She liked the woman immediately, summing her up as eccentric but nice.

Colin, well versed in the passenger list, said charmingly, "Lady Travitt, I am delighted to meet you. I have hesitated to thrust a young man's attentions upon you, but—"

"What do you think I want – an old man's?" Elvira rasped. She shook his hand briefly. She didn't like the pushing kind. And he needn't think he can win me over with that disarming smile, she thought sagely, and the next minute found herself inviting the pair of them to join her.

"Deck steward is just coming round with a tray. I

imagine you'll be glad of refreshment after that strenuous exercise. You know Doctor Halliday, of course?"

Mike shook Patsy's hand, then nodded to Butler.

"We haven't met before, but your face is familiar."

"That's more than likely. I have travelled on this vessel many times. Fortunately, I have never needed your services."

"You may yet," Elvira croaked. "Weather forecast is bad. Very bad."

"That won't worry me. I'm a good sailor."

Patsy said ruefully that it would worry *her*. "I was ill the first day out, and the sea wasn't really rough at all."

Elvira assured her that the doctor had good medical supplies. "As well as a capable new nurse," she added. "Charming, too." She finished with a significant glance toward Colin.

"Oh, we know her!" Patsy put in. "She was wonderful to me when I was praying for the *Regina* to sink to the ocean bed and stay there. And she's an old friend of Colin's."

"Indeed? She has nursed you, perhaps, Mr. Butler?"

"No. I've known her personally for some time."

"Then what a coincidence she came on this ship!"

"Yes, isn't it?" he agreed pleasantly.

The arrival of the deck steward broke up the conversation. Patsy drank beef tea with the healthy appetite of the young, and Elvira with the frank appreciation of the old. Mike touched the peak of his nautical cap in a farewell salute and said, "I must get back to work," ignoring Elvira's command to stay. The arrogant confidence of Colin Butler jarred on him and he found himself remembering that first night out, when he had seen Lesley in the man's arms.

He turned away abruptly and went below to his own

quarters. He wasn't needed in the surgery this morning. If an emergency cropped up they would ring through to him, so he resolved to make the most of this opportunity to get on with his book.

But it didn't go nearly so well as he hoped.

Patsy floated lazily on her back. Warm sea water, heated to exactly the right temperature, lapped her body. She had never seen a swimming pool so beautiful as this and her eyes scanned the glistening walls and roof with frank wonder. She had read all about it before the *Regina* sailed, of course. She'd had plenty of time to, for she was one of the first passengers to come aboard and in the luxury of her stateroom she had scanned the information book eagerly. She could even have quoted statistics, but knew that if she did so Colin would regard it as odd.

What would he say were she to announce that the walls surrounding this magnificent indoor pool were covered with a latex composition filled with mother-of-pearl chippings, the polished surface interlaced with wavy metal strips of bronze to achieve the effect of an underwater scene? He would smile indulgently, but with that faintly puzzled air she had detected once or twice this afternoon – as if, in some way, he couldn't quite understand her.

She was anxious not to awaken the slightest doubt or suspicion in his mind. It would never do to let him know the truth – not at this stage, anyway. The time for truth had been at the very beginning, before they got to know each other, and certainly before they became important to each other. Because they *were* important to each other now, weren't they? Those interchanged glances, those moments of startling recognition, the feeling of having known each other for a long time – and the contrasting feeling that they had been waiting to meet each other even longer – were too potent and disturbing to be without significance.

She rolled over and began a leisurely breast stroke. Beneath her she could see the glistening sea-green mosaic of the pool's base, matching the tall columns, like Grecian pillars, which flanked the water's edge. Concealed lighting filtered through the clear water, giving a translucent effect.

They had the pool entirely to themselves. She was glad of that. She wanted to have the rest of this enchanted day alone with him. Tonight there would be more dancing and more festivity. She would wear the white tulle, sequin-scattered, which she had bought as a final reckless purchase. When would she get the chance to wear it again, after this one trip into Wonderland? Perhaps never. But what did it matter? She would have the dream to remember – and Colin along with it.

Beneath the magic, sadness touched her. She hadn't meant to fall in love. She didn't want to. Love complicated things and she wanted to retain a memory of untroubled enjoyment. She'd had the whole thing mapped out in her mind; the cost (financial) assessed to the last detail. Not for a moment had she considered that there might be another reckoning to be made, concerning her heart.

Colin's strong arms clasped her waist, pulling her beneath the water with him. They submerged swiftly, surfacing seconds later face to face and laughing boisterously. She swept the wet hair from her eyes, turned on to her back again, and pedalled water vigorously all over him. His laughing protest echoed between the marble pillars and he swam after her, threatening revenge.

He caught her as she climbed from the pool, but she broke free and raced for the diving board. He seized her slim ankle as she climbed the steps, and held it. "Now you're my prisoner! I can hold you to ransom or toss you to the deep! Which shall it be?'' For answer, she tried to kick free and fell headlong into his arms.

It was over in a moment – the sudden embrace, the swift and impassioned kiss, the mutual desire. Then she broke free and ran away, her heart beating in an unfamiliar and frightening fashion. He was flirting with her – how could it be anything else? – but her young and untried heart was incapable of resistance. She had fallen in love with him and despite the magic of it she was aware of an overpowering desire to cry.

Back in her stateroom she was hardly aware of the tears which ran unheeded down her face. There was a wild happiness within her, but a sadness too; a kind of mourning for the fate which made a girl fall in love with the wrong man.

Because he undoubtedly was the wrong man. She knew that with the certainty and wisdom acquired in a tough school. Life had taught Patsy to recognise people for what they were worth and somewhere, somehow, Colin's character had wavered, his sense of values had gone awry. She saw him for what he was, but it didn't make her love him any the less.

There's nothing to be done about it, she reflected unhappily. I've got to go on until the end, hiding the truth and relishing every moment with him until we say goodbye.

The dressmaking session went well. It was quiet in the surgery that afternoon; like the lull before the storm, Walker commented wryly, and as if to confirm his words the *Regina* began to pitch at about five o'clock – slightly at first, not enough to bother anyone, but enough to make Maude and Lesley glad that the dress was cut out before the table began to roll with the motion of the ship.

Maude carried the dress away to her cabin, to tack together on Lesley's instructions. Reaching the lower deck she saw Colin and Patsy descending from the tea lounge. The girl looked as attractive as ever in a green linen pantsuit, her hair freshly styled and set after her swim. She was gazing at her companion with unabashed pleasure and Maude mentally shook her wise head.

My, my, the girl *has* got it badly! Swiftly, too. Now I wonder what the end of *that* affair will be? Good gracious, I'm becoming as bad as old Lady Travitt!

Even so, curiosity held her. She saw Colin's face as he gazed down on Patsy and guessed at once that the attraction was by no means one-sided. Maude smiled at them benignly as they passed. Young people in love always touched her heart.

The next person she saw was Elvira Travitt, watching the couple with frank curiosity whilst pretending to study the ship's course from an immense electrically-operated chart upon a nearby wall. Maude knew well enough that Elvira had no interest whatsoever in latitude or longitude or how many knots the ship travelled, and at her sceptical glance Elvira shook her dyed head in unabashed agreement.

"You're right, my dear – it doesn't mean a thing to me. I am spying on those two, and they're so wrapped up in each other they aren't even aware of it! A good thing your Nurse Owen isn't around to see them!"

"Why?" asked Maude, in surprise.

"Because, as I told our pig-headed doctor, that young man is the reason for her being on this ship. Didn't you know? She has come after him."

"My dear Lady Travitt, I'm sure you are wrong. Lesley took this job because she needed it. I happen to know that."

"And *I* happen to know that she was not only acquainted with that handsome young devil before she came aboard, but that the job was merely an excuse to be near him. And," Elvira finished with injured dignity, "I am *never* wrong, Sister."

Maude gave an indulgent smile and went on her way, but she was a little out of patience with Lady Travitt, who could be tiresome enough when spying on the ship's passengers and making wild guesses about them, without extending the activity to ship's personnel – especially medical personnel.

But what was it the old woman had said – that she had told Mike Halliday this ridiculous tale about Lesley? If so, he would be calling the girl a husband-hunter next, if he hadn't done so already. Maude sighed and decided to think about it no more.

Feeling better for the decision, she reached her cabin and settled down happily to her sewing, glad she was off duty this evening. By bedtime she would have all these seams tacked and ready for machining. There were sewing machines in the valet and service department; she could easily borrow one. She put her feet up and relaxed. It was wonderful to be free for a whole evening, a luxury she had never enjoyed until Lesley came aboard. Always she had been on call, wherever she was and whatever the hour, but now she could be sure of undisturbed privacy unless an unexpected run of emergencies demanded the attention of both nurses.

As if to discourage optimism the *Regina* gave a long and shuddering roll, pitching her massive weight against the power of the sea, then settling down into a trough as steep as the foothill of a mountain. The next moment she was climbing out of it, poised for another descent which came all too soon and all too sickeningly. It was like the lifting of a giant hand with the massive vessel held like a toy within its palm. Maude's needle paused, arrested. So it was coming, the break in her leisure. She had indeed been too optimistic.

After another gigantic roll the vessel went serenely on its way, but Sister Collard was not deceived. Throughout the length and breadth of the *Regina* hundreds of relieved sighs were no doubt being uttered at that very moment, but she was a seasoned voyager and knew the signs. That toying with the elements had been a forerunner of worse to come, and sooner or later it would overtake them.

Maude's needle flew with philosophical determination. She wasn't going to be cheated out of this new dress by any meteorological whim; she wanted to wear it in New York, where she sometimes visited international nurses' clubs. It was about time she showed them something new, she thought wryly.

After all, it was a false alarm. The promised storm sent out no more threatening signs and the passengers settled down to enjoy the rest of the day. After tea, Patsy and Colin went to see a new film – one which had not yet been shown even in London. The Owen Line paid highly for such rights and ensured that their clients saw the film in supreme comfort. Seating was luxurious, upholstery of red velvet on chairs designed to give the maximum ease. Carpets of deep blue covered the sloping floor and from ivory walls small lighthouse lenses made decorative spots. Curtains of crimson velvet, patterned with silver, screened the stage, which was sometimes used for concerts and was flanked by massed flowers and shrubs.

This time Patsy managed to suppress a sigh of wonder. She was rapidly acquiring a more sophisticated appreciation of the *Regina's* luxury and with every passing minute was less likely to betray herself. She was aware of the fact without being comforted by it. If anything should happen between herself and Colin, if anything serious should develop out of their friendship, the truth would come out anyway. It would have to. Basically she was absolutely honest, and had embarked upon this adventure without dreaming that it could lead to anything more than the most exciting experience of her life.

The film was good, but she paid little attention to it. Nor did Colin. An awareness was growing between them which was stronger than mere flirtation, more durable than passing attraction. It was like a tenuous thread weaving a chain between their hearts, binding them irrevocably. Colin was disturbed by it; even a little frightened because it threatened to be something he could not control and such an experience was new to him.

In the darkness his hand reached out to her and, without turning her head, Patsy sensed the movement. Swiftly, her fingers met his, intertwined, and remained there passively. And so they sat, hand in hand, until the film was over and the miniature lighthouses dispelled the darkness, bringing them back to reality again.

They were silent as they left the cinema; silent as they went below to change for dinner. Not until they reached the door of Patsy's stateroom did Colin speak. "You'll meet me before dinner, won't you – but not in the Observation Lounge this time. The bar there is too crowded. Make it the starboard winter garden. We can be almost alone there . . . "

She nodded her agreement, almost shyly, he felt, and went within. Her door closed and, as it did so, an adjoining one opened. Colin turned at the sound and saw the raddled face of a rather bizarre old woman looking at him. He recognised her as Lady Travitt and flashed his disarming smile. In reply she said briskly, "I want a word with you, young man. Come inside," and before he knew what was happening he was obeying her.

He walked into one of the most expensive suites the *Regina* had to offer, wondering what on earth its occupant could want to talk to him about and thinking how unfair it was that someone too old to relish all this luxury could afford to pay several hundred pounds a day for it, probably without even counting the cost.

After commanding him to close the door, Elvira said abruptly, "Young man, leave that girl alone. It's her money you're after, and I know it. But *she* doesn't. How would she react if I told her, do you think?"

A dull colour mounted his face.

"I don't know what you are talking about – "

"Oh yes, you do. The little girl next door, the one with all the beautiful clothes. Money no object, obviously."

He answered almost truculently, "Perhaps that's why she doesn't flaunt it – because she is accustomed to it. In any case, I can't see what business it is of yours."

"None at all, and I know it. But my own business is well looked after by solicitors and accountants, so there's nothing else for me to do but to look after other people's." Elvira gave her dry cackle. "It's much more enjoyable, too. The looker-on sees most of the game, you know. That's why I see yours."

He said frigidly, "If you will excuse me, Lady Travitt, I must change for dinner . . . "

"Oh, *I'll* excuse you, but will Lesley, do you think? Will she excuse or understand your pursuit of little Miss Davis? I doubt it. Because she came on this voyage to be near you, didn't she?"

"*How do you know?*"

The parrot-like face grinned mischievously.

"Guesswork mostly. That, and a shrewd suspicion that her surname, being the same as that of the Owen Line's Chairman, is more than mere coincidence. I have a hunch, Mr. Butler, and I always back my hunches. I am backing this one. How did Miss Owen get this nursing job aboard the *Regina*, and why? I can think of ways and reasons."

"You think a great deal too much, Lady Travitt."

"You can be as rude to me as you like, my boy. I am always rude myself, and enjoy it, so of course I must excuse the fault in others. All the same, take my advice. Go after the nurse. Stick to the certainty. It's safer."

Colin, who had half opened the door, shut it again with a sharp little slam and came back into the room. She was surprised by the anger in his face.

"Listen to me," he said tensely. "I'm a lot more shrewd than you think. I can see through people too, and I see through you. You're the kind of shipboard passenger who delights in making mischief and spreading rumour. You're a menace."

"I know," she agreed happily.

"So I am not in the least likely to heed you."

"A pity. I did so want you to stick to the nurse."

He controlled himself with an effort. The desire to shake this meddlesome old woman was almost frightening in its urgency. She was too perceptive by far. She had guessed the truth about Lesley somehow, but obviously knew as little about Patsy as he did. One truth only had she come out with – that the girl had money.

He said abruptly, "I'll handle my own affairs in my own way, Lady Travitt."

The dyed head, tipped a little to one side, studied him with the pert curiosity of a sparrow.

"You're very confident, young man. But don't be over confident. And, if you are, don't say I didn't warn you . . ."

He spun away from her. He had no time for garrulous old women who could be of no possible use to him. He felt sorry for the old girl, of course. A bit nutty, but so long as she kept her imagination under control and her nose out of other people's affairs, that could do no harm. Even so, he didn't like her references to Lesley because they made him feel uncomfortable.

He halted at the door. "If I've been rude, I apologise." Then curiosity made him add, "What was it you really wanted to say to me?"

The mascaraed eyes opened in surprise.

"I've said it, haven't I?"

"I don't think you have, somehow. In fact, I'm sure you have *not*."

CHAPTER EIGHT

At half past seven Lesley left the surgery and made her way to the dining room. It was a calm, clear evening and a breath of air before dinner appealed to her. So she made a detour to the promenade deck and, in so doing, passed through the starboard garden lounge where Colin and Patsy were enjoying an aperitif together, side by side upon a wicker garden seat.

Neither saw her. They were too engrossed in each other, though neither was saying a word. Patsy wasn't even looking at Colin; she was twirling the small cocktail glass in her hands and watching the amber liquid within it, but even an unprejudiced observer would have known that she was aware only of the man at her side; the man who was regarding her lovely profile with the intentness of a lover.

Not being an unprejudiced observer, Lesley saw a great deal more. She sensed the atmosphere between them and recognised the cause because it was so painfully familiar. Colin had once looked at herself in the same fashion, monopolising her and making love to her with every glance.

Swiftly and silently she crossed the terraced floor and went out on deck. They didn't even notice her. They were isolated in a world of their own.

Lesley found a sheltered corner and withdrew into it, lifting her face to the evening air and breathing deeply to steady herself. She couldn't blame Colin, because

Patsy was so lovely, and she couldn't blame Patsy, because Colin was so attractive. And they were both travelling alone, so what if they *were* flirting a little? It could mean nothing, like most shipboard flirtations.

That was why her own affair with Colin had been so different. It had been more than an *affaire* even at the beginning.

So she had to be sensible about this. She mustn't imagine things of which she had no proof. She mustn't misread small things or misinterpret glances. And, above all, she must not be jealous.

She decided to return by the garden lounge and to greet them quite naturally, but when she reached it again they had gone. There was nothing but a pair of empty cocktail glasses on a table to remind her that they had been there at all.

Maude was already seated when Lesley entered the dining room.

"The doctor isn't here yet," she said. "What was he doing when you left the surgery?"

"Paper work at his desk. I expect he'll be along when he finishes."

Conversation was an effort. Lesley's glance kept wandering across the vast room, searching in vain for a glimpse of Colin. Once she thought she saw Patsy's shining head rising like a flower from a cloud-like dress in which scattered sequins gleamed like distant stars, but at this hour the place was crowded and busy stewards constantly obstructed the view. Lesley gave up, finished her dinner quickly, and returned to work.

Evening duty meant that she had to stand by until eleven, later calls being put through to her cabin. There seemed no possibility of an interruption tonight, however. All was quiet. The *Regina* was steady on her course again and the evening promised nothing more exciting than a quiet spell in the surgery with a library book.

Mike was still at his desk when she entered. He glanced up, nodded briefly, and returned to his work. She crossed to the dispensary and he said over his shoulder, "There's no need to isolate yourself in there. I'm just going down for dinner . . ."

He pushed his work aside and left without glancing at her. After he had gone, the surgery still held the imprint of his personality and she had the feeling that no matter how long he might vacate the place it would still be dominated by him. It was then that she realised just how strong an impression this man could make, not only on people, but on places. Pioneers must have been made of the same stuff, she thought, leaving their marks behind.

Mike Halliday was certainly disturbing. She found it necessary to forcibly dismiss him from her mind, but solitary duty hours were too easily invaded by thought. She moved restlessly about the room, making a pretence of tidying where no tidying was necessary, and resisting the almost overwhelming temptation to cross to his desk, to sit down in front of it, to put out her hands and lay them where, a short while ago, his own had rested. She wanted nothing so much as to occupy his chair, to handle his possessions, to pick up the pen which must still be warm from his touch, to turn the pages on which he had been writing and which must bear the unseen impression of his long, sensitive fingers.

Instinctively, she did so. As she thought, the pen was still warm from his touch. She had no right to open the folder on his desk, or to examine his work, yet she did. His writing was strong and forceful, exactly the sort of writing she expected to see.

The door opened abruptly and her head jerked round. Caught like a guilty schoolgirl, she sat there with the pen in her hand, looking at the doctor in a rush of embarrassment.

He stared, then demanded, "What the devil are you doing at my desk?"

Words failed her. She could hardly admit that she had wanted to touch his papers, sit in his chair, feel his pen between her fingers, or that she was curious to see his handwriting and try to interpret his character from it. So she took a deep breath and said frankly, "I wondered what work you were engaged on, Doctor. Are you writing a book?"

Her cool effrontery startled him. That she had no right to sit at his desk and examine his papers she must very well know, and a tell-tale flush in her cheeks confirmed this — then an unwilling admiration replaced his annoyance. She wasn't a coward, anyway. She didn't offer excuses or evasions.

"Yes, Nurse, I am. But I doubt if it would interest you. It is merely a report of some medical research I've been carrying out in my spare time for a number of years, entirely for my own interest. I doubt if any medical publisher would share it. I have no distinction to lend weight to my theories or findings."

She wanted to protest that he was too young to have won distinction yet, which meant, of course, that she believed he would one day achieve it.

She laid down his pen and moved away, but again his tall figure blocked her path. The strength and breadth and height of the man overwhelmed her as before, so that she could do nothing but stand there, waiting for him to move aside.

He remained looking down at her, his face revealing nothing although his feelings were in turmoil. He had resolved, long ago, to be wary of all women and never to let them touch his heart again, but now he was aware of Lesley Owen in an increasing and alarming fashion.

She stammered, "I'm sure some publisher will be interested in your book . . . " but her voice trailed away, silencing abruptly as his arms went round her and his mouth came down on hers.

He kissed her with passion, the strength of his grasp making escape impossible. Not that she wanted to escape. She was unresisting and helpless.

He continued to kiss her until her senses reeled. His sudden release caused her to sway. She was thankful for the solid desk behind her and for a full minute remained there, gripping the edge with both hands and seeing the doctor's bitter mouth smiling down at her.

"I suppose I ought to apologise for that, but I won't. If a passenger is permitted to make love to you on the boat deck, why shouldn't I, in the surgery? You wanted me to the last time, didn't you?"

His words stung her into action. Shame and anger sent her hand flashing out, striking his face. He laughed, caught her wrist and held it, pulling her towards him until he pinioned her body close to his own. Furiously she beat against his chest, but he only laughed the more.

"You can't escape, Nurse, so you can give up the struggle. Be still, you little fool, while I kiss you again."

She sobbed with impotent fury, but her sobs were silenced by a kiss which was infinitely tender but profoundly stirring with its promise of greater passion, until she lay quietly in his arms and the madly spinning world revolved more slowly, steadying down to an even keel again.

He laid his cheek against her hair. "I'm sorry," he said hoarsely. "Forgive me, Lesley—"

Sanity returned. She pushed him away and fled to the dispensary, slamming the door behind her, but in that moment of violent withdrawal he saw something which surprised him — her cheeks were wet.

He passed a trembling hand across his eyes, shaking his head briefly as if to clear his brain. He must have been mad! But the quality of his madness was very revealing — he was mad with jealousy and resentment and honest-to-goodness masculine desire, which was an extraordinary way to feel about a girl he disliked . . .

Lesley leaned against the dispensary door and closed her eyes. She covered her face with her hands and felt the tears hot on her fingers. Humiliation vied with anger, but more predominant was a sense of shame because she had experienced a moment of complete surrender. Loving Colin as she did, to feel such an overriding response to another man's ardour seemed totally disloyal, quite apart from the surprise of discovering that another man *could* arouse her in such a way.

Fury with herself vied with fury against the doctor. I hate him, *hate* him! I hate his conceit and his egoism and his brute vitality! I hate his injustice and his cruelty and I won't work another voyage with him!

But she couldn't quit the ship at New York. There was the whole cruise ahead — Florida, Puerto Rico, the Virgin Isles, Martinique, Venezuela, Aruba, Curaçao, Jamaica and Haiti; all those exotic places with their blue horizons which had spread so enticingly before her when she had visualised herself enjoying them with Colin, but she had reckoned without the intrusion of a disturbing personality like Mike Halliday.

Underlying her stormy emotions was frank astonishment at his behaviour. Who would have dreamed that so cold a man could be capable of such passion? Tenderness, too. The touch of his lips still lay on her own, warm with a pressure which was at once gentle and lovely.

She rubbed her mouth with the back of her hand, trying vainly to obliterate even the memory of that touch, but the emotional impact of those moments had been real and important to her; how important and in what way she refused to understand, turning her back on reason because to face the truth was something she dared not do.

She had always believed that she possessed self-control, but now she was not so sure. To ignore her leaping response to the man was impossible; it had been there, strong and potent and compelling. And why had he kissed her in the first place? Had it been deliberate and calculated, a trick to prove her unworthy of her position and so justify her dismissal? If so, the trick was despicable and so was he for indulging in it.

But in his final withdrawal, hadn't there been a quality of surprise which matched her own?

She sat down slowly and thoughtfully, acknowledging to herself that the moment in his arms had been beautiful, and for this reason she had to forget it. The only way to do that was by remembering the bitter accusation of his voice and the stinging contempt of his words. If she clung to that memory her dislike of him would be maintained, and in that way she would feel safe and unchallenged again.

All was quiet back in the surgery. That meant he had gone. She wondered why he had returned in the first place and what excuse he would have offered, had one been necessary.

She opened the dividing door. As she expected, the place was empty. She hoped he would not come back and that the next time she faced him they would not be alone.

Mike was hoping the same thing. Hurrying from the surgery, he regained his quarters before he remembered that his pen, for which he had gone back, still lay on his desk. She had been holding it, he recalled, and now he wondered why. She had wanted to borrow it, perhaps, to make some official entry and that was also the reason for sitting at his desk. He had been a hot-headed fool to fly off the handle like that when he saw her seated there.

Hot-headed in more ways than one. Hot-blooded, too. The strength of his passion left him shaken and surprised. Such an effect was the last he had ever expected Lesley Owen to have on him; he had been armed against her from the beginning, but now his confidence in that armour, and in himself, had suffered a jolt.

He would have to apologise, of course, choosing a better moment than he had done – although he was not in the least sorry that he had kissed her. His only regret was that he had been weak enough to do so, and he had to remember that she was in love with someone else. What Elvira predicted usually came true; her observations were usually proved sound. But now he remembered that Lesley had returned his kisses with an instinctive abandonment which was not the normal behaviour of a girl in love with another man. True, she had put up some sort of resistance at first, but it had quickly broken down. So what did that mean? That she was highly sexed and incapable of resisting a man's overtures – or that she was not in love as deeply as Elvira believed?

He hoped Sister Collard would have finished dining by the time he joined her, and was glad to observe the empty table. He wanted to be alone; he wanted to think, to take stock of himself, to analyse his extraordinary behaviour. He was aware that it had been prompted by something more than physical desire, though heaven

125

knew that had been there too, but what that extra some-thing was, he refused to believe.

Walker looked into the surgery shortly before eleven.

"All present and correct, Nurse?" he asked cheerfully.

"I thought you were off duty," Lesley answered.

"So I am, but a bit browned off. Don't like these in-active crossings. Lots of bodies strewn around the place, plenty of patients – that's what I like. So long as I'm not one of 'em!"

She laughed.

"You're callous, Walker."

"Not really, Nurse. I just like to keep busy. Doc's the same. Haven't you noticed?"

"I can't say I have. I can't say I've noticed the doctor particularly, in any way at all."

His shrewd Cockney face regarded her sceptically.

"Now that I *don't* believe, Nurse, seeing as 'ow the doctor's the kinda bloke anyone'd notice, like him or not. He just can't be overlooked. You either likes 'im or loathes 'im, but there's no not-noticing-'im!"

She changed the subject.

"Are you wanting something?" she asked. He was off duty, so his visit was unexpected.

"Yes – a bit of company. Someone to talk to, other than the stewards or the shop assistants or the bank clerks or the barmen or the Purser's staff. Passengers don't mix much with the likes o' me, except down in Tourist, and that's too far to walk. Besides, I'm sort'f attached to this surgery. It's my home when aboard, as it were." He looked at her with a fatherly concern which seemed out of keeping with his cheerful monkey's face. "Feeling all right, Nurse? Not 'omesick, I mean, or lonely?"

She assured him that she was fine, to which he re-marked that she didn't look it. "You look kinda peaked, to me. Why don't you go aloft for a breather? The night is young."

"I will when I go off duty." She added with interest, glad of his company as greatly as he was glad of hers, "Tell me about yourself, Walker."

"There isn't much to tell, reely. I'm an ordinary sorta bloke, with a flat in Streatham and a wife and a coupla kids. Nice kids. Like to see 'em?"

"I would indeed." She studied a well-thumbed snapshot with interest. "This is your wife with them, of course."

"Yes. Nice looker, ain't she?"

"Very nice. You must miss her."

"You bet I do. That's one of the reasons I come to sea."

"I don't understand . . . "

"Simple! Life's a run of honeymoons when you're apart for as long as we are. These voyages are just long enough for me to get thoroughly 'omesick and to make 'er miss me good'n proper, so when we get together again – wow! Those spells back 'ome are something to live for, I can tell you, and never time for a cross word between us – and the kids see more of me then than other kids see of their dads from one month's end to another, I reckon, seeing as 'ow I'm there all the time until we sail again. Then there's the next time round to look forward to, and all my money saved up for it – and I'm back, putting my key in the front door, before she 'as time to miss me so much that she's comforting 'erself with some other bloke!"

Lesley laughed. "Well, that's *one* good recipe for a happy marriage! But you said 'one of the reasons' – is there another?"

"The doctor, o' course."

That surprised her.

"Doctor Halliday! But why?"

.." 'E brought me to sea in the first place; it was 'e wot persuaded me. Didn't you know? I was an orderly at St. Giles's – that's the 'ospital 'e trained at."

"So you've known him a long time?"

"*I'll* say! When 'e qualified 'e was all set to take over 'is father's practice in Sussex – comes of a medical family, y'see – and Mabel and I and the kids were all set to go along with 'em. He was getting married and we were going to live and work for 'em, both of us, me as 'andyman and the wife on the domestic side ..."

"Then – why didn't you go?"

" 'Cos 'e didn't get married."

She wanted to ask why, and couldn't, but she wondered who the girl had been.

"What happened?" she asked.

Walker shrugged.

"Don't ask me! I dunno. Suddenly the whole thing was off and 'is brother took over the family practice instead, and the next thing I knew, Doc. 'Alliday'd signed on for this job. So I did, too. I've always suspected 'e persuaded 'em to take me on, 'cos it isn't easy just to step into jobs like this."

"You mean he pulled strings? I thought he frowned on that sort of thing!"

"Oh, I dunno about that, Nurse. Shouldn't think so, seeing as 'ow 'e was new to the Line, but I think 'e recommended me and said how 'e'd like to 'ave me along with 'im. That goes for me, too. I like working alongside the doctor."

"In fact, you like the doctor himself."

"Like 'im! I think the world of 'im, Nurse, and so will you, one day."

Lesley turned away, asking casually, "Who was the girl he was to marry, and why didn't he?"

"I dunno. Never met 'er. 'E used to speak of 'er as Carol, but who she was and why they didn't marry, I've no idea."

The surgery, kept at normal room heat, seemed suddenly close. Lesley glanced at the thermometer and said, "The temperature is going up. I wonder why."

"Storm coming up, probably."

"It was forecast, but there was no more than a preliminary skirmish. Now the sea is as calm as a millpond, isn't it?"

"*Too* calm. It's the lull before the storm, believe me. Why don't you take a turn on deck, Nurse, while you've got a chance? You'll be rushed off your feet if it breaks. I'll stand by till you come back."

"That's kind of you. I'll take your advice."

She was glad to get above decks. People in evening dress strolled together, or danced to the distant strains of music from the ballroom. Heading towards the stern, Lesley glanced through the windows, pausing involuntarily to admire the glittering scene. The colour of the women's gowns, the magpie effect of men's evening wear, the splashes of white made by the tropical dinner jackets which more and more male passengers seemed to be appearing in, presented a colourful picture. It was hard to believe that she was looking into a ballroom hundreds of miles from land; a floating palace in mid-ocean. The scene was reminiscent of some fabulous hotel on the Riviera, and even as she thought this, a couple glided into her vision; a couple who held each other very closely.

Lesley recognised them at once, although she could scarcely see their features; the man's cheek rested against the girl's, concealing her face, but Lesley recognised not only that sylph-like figure, but that handsome male profile.

She turned on her heel and walked briskly along the deck. She walked the full length of it three times, and not once did she glance through those windows again. Before going below, she stood at the ship's rail for awhile, gazing out to sea. There were things which had to be faced, and the sooner she began facing them, the better. The first was that nothing had worked out as planned. Her uncle had spoken the truth when declaring that as a member of ship's personnel she would have little opportunity to be with Colin, but what he had not predicted was that Colin would make little opportunity to see her. Had he wanted to, he could have done so any time. He could have rung through to the surgery this evening, and even joined her there for a while. It was against the rules, but Sister would have turned a blind eye. She had even hinted so. "So long as visitors don't drop in when we are busy, that is all that matters, Nurse." But Colin had not dropped in at all because he had been engrossed with someone else almost from the time they sailed.

Turning to go below, she saw them coming along the deck, walking in the moonlight together, unaware of anyone or anything but themselves.

She headed for the nearest companion way and descended before they reached her. Her haste was unnecessary, for in their absorption neither would have seen her.

CHAPTER NINE

By now Patsy had resigned herself to the inevitable. She had fallen in love with Colin Butler and there was nothing she could do about it. In time, perhaps, it would subside into nothing more than a dull ache which might trouble her during solitary hours back in the Dulwich bed-sit, but she was sensible enough to know that life for anyone as young and pretty as herself would certainly go on and, no doubt, offer her other opportunities, other men, other occasions to fall in love.

But what sort of men? None to compare with Colin; none with his experience and sophistication and social graces – unless, of course, she won another beauty contest. But the going was hard in that particular world with every competitor fighting to reach the peak, to be Miss World. Patsy knew that, pretty as she was, her chance of winning an event like that was remote.

All the same, she wasn't grumbling. Life had given her this much, which was more than it gave to many, and if all she had was a broken heart at the end of it, she had no one to blame but herself. She could have tucked the money away in the bank and hardly known it was there, but the comforting knowledge that she had invested it sensibly and safely wouldn't have given her the pleasure this voyage had given her.

Sometimes she found it hard to realise that it was really she who paced this vast and splendid deck with a handsome man, that it was she who occupied that luxurious stateroom and lingered over a prolonged toilet night and morning and whenever she wished in between; that it was she who opened the vast cupboards and selected the right clothes for the right occasion, in the certain knowledge that she couldn't possibly go wrong for any event. It was all a dream and one from which she would waken with a jerk.

Meanwhile, she was more than willing to prolong it. She had firmly decided that it would be better to say goodbye to Colin at the end of it, and never to see him again. She had her own reasons for this decision, and knew it to be the right one.

So she made no resistance when he kissed her. Why should she? She was free, and there was no other woman in his life to whom he owed loyalty. Once, she had asked him lightly, "Am I treading on anyone's toes, Colin? I mean, are you married or anything?"

"I don't know what you mean by 'or anything', but the answer is no."

She believed him because she wanted to believe him, and because on the face of it he didn't seem the kind of man to deliberately lie. He had his faults – who hadn't? – and, like herself, his weaknesses, but fundamentally he wasn't bad in the true sense of the word. And even if he had been, her loyal little heart would still have loved him.

So she kissed him without any inhibition. Her upbringing had laid no veneer upon her; she was neither afraid nor ashamed of revealing her heart. She was a simple and uncomplicated person, spontaneous in her affection and grateful for the bounty a generous fate had dropped into her lap.

"Do you realise we have only two more nights like this?" he whispered. "Two more days before we see New York harbour?"

She realised it only too well.

"Why don't you stay on for the rest of the cruise?" he urged. "Why stop off at New York?"

Because that's as far as my budget takes me, she wanted to say. At the daily rate this luxury costs, even five thousand won't take me the whole round trip ... But aloud she merely answered, "Let's enjoy ourselves while we can."

"But we'll see each other in New York, won't we? Where are you staying? I must have your phone number, don't forget."

"I'm – not sure yet."

"With relatives, perhaps?"

"No—"

He looked at her curiously. "Tell me about yourself, Patsy."

"There's nothing to tell. I'm just an ordinary person—"

"Not you. Ordinary girls don't look like you."

He made it a simple statement of fact, without any suggestion of flattery. In any case, she knew it to be true, and felt no conceit about it. Fate gave some girls brains, others wealth, but to her it had given looks. And looks didn't last for ever, she thought philosophically, so she'd better make the most of them for now ...

"Let's dance, Colin. All night – or at any rate until the band stops playing."

There was a kind of desperate gaiety about her. His blue eyes studied her with disturbing penetration.

"I'd rather stay on deck with you, Patsy."

"But it's turning chilly – and there's a breeze getting up—"

"It's nothing. It will pass."

But there he was wrong. The breeze became a wind, gathering momentum with astonishing speed. White crests appeared on the calm millpond of the ocean and the vast wake of the ship was soon a maelstrom. Patsy shivered and Colin put a protective arm about her shoulders.

"You're right," he said. "It's getting up with a vengeance! Let's go below. There'll be some games going on in the main lounge – have you played that racing game the lounge steward organises every night? Better still, we could go along to the smoking lounge where the millionaires bet on the ship's speed every evening. Just to listen to them tossing away thousands without batting an eyelid is an education in itself! Not that *you* need educating in any way."

Oh, but I do, she thought sadly, remembering the comprehensive school she had gone to and her modest O Levels.

They took a lift down to the main hall, passing through the magnificent lounge on their way to the smoking room. Elvira was there, but Colin pretended not to see her. Reaching the smoking room he found an unoccupied table facing the forward bulkhead, on which was a vast chart, electrically operated, showing the minute-by-minute position of the *Regina*. Below it, on a rostrum, sat the smoking room steward, with an auctioneer's hammer in his hand. He conducted the betting as an auctioneer conducted a sale. From all parts of the walnut-panelled room immaculately dressed men called their bets and, to Patsy's amazement, the figures ran into many thousands.

"Fantastic, isn't it?" Colin said. "Fortunes are won and lost here every night. I've heard tell that some of these men 'play the run' on every alternate Atlantic crossing; it's their way of making a living, free of tax because out here in mid-ocean they're outside the bounds of jurisdiction. In between, they take a couple of weeks off, living in luxury ashore at either end. It's all perfectly legal. No betting laws govern a ship at sea."

"And what happens to those who *lose* the fortunes? Surely nobody is rich enough to risk bankruptcy overnight? These men, these people bandying their thousands so recklessly, are they as rich as all that?"

"Some of them. Others hope to be. The wise ones stop when they reach a certain limit. But I can understand the thrill of it, the temptation."

"Well, I can't," Patsy said practically, then realised that her own action, if on a smaller scale, had not been so very different. She had won – and spent it all. But at least, she thought defiantly, I didn't throw it away! I did get something for it – an experience I would never have had otherwise, and a wardrobe which will last me a good long time. And who knows? Some of these clothes may land me a good job when I get home. I'll be well dressed when I go for interviews . . .

"Do you envy the rich, Colin?"

"Of course I do."

"Why?"

He shrugged. He found the question hard to answer.

"I suppose – because money can buy things. Comforts and luxuries and world-wide travel. Things like that. I won't be content to represent Baynards for ever. I'd like to be higher up."

"The best way to get higher is to climb there, and that means hard work. Unless, of course, you plan to marry for money."

He asked sharply, "What do you mean?"

"Simply that that's one good way of climbing, an easy way. A man can buy himself a good position, even a partnership, providing he can lay his hands on the means."

He was surprised to feel a dull tide of shame spreading through him. He seized her hand and said abruptly, "Let's go and dance."

She went with him silently. Had he known it, she felt too sick at heart to say another word. She had been a fool to fall in love with this man, and he had been a fool to develop such a wrong sense of values, and there was nothing she could do about any of it.

Outside, he slipped an arm about her waist. "No more seriousness!" he said gaily. "Let's make the most of every moment, let's enjoy ourselves!"

Her only response was a forced little smile which he had no time to notice because at that precise moment the ship gave a sudden roll, hurling her against him. Before they could steady themselves, it had lurched again more violently, and within a matter of minutes the threatening storm was on them in full force.

"Are you all right, Patsy?"

"Of course—"

"Not frightened?"

"Should I be?"

"Some people are – look at them!"

He was right. Passengers were hurrying to their cabins, lurching from wall to wall, or clinging helplessly to handrails. When the *Regina* rolled she rolled with a vengeance, shifting the great walls of the Atlantic with no mean force. She was too vast, too big, too heavy to ride the waves. She ploughed her way through them with drunken abandon.

"Want to turn in, Patsy?"

"Of course not! I feel fine! Let's dance – or try to!"

He laughed. She was a game little thing, and his determination to make this night a memorable one increased. "We'll have the time of our lives," he promised, and steered her towards the lifts. He managed to lead her into one despite the rolling deck beneath them, and it wasn't until they reached the ballroom level that the accident happened. By then, the ship was pitching heavily and, to keep the lift gate open as Patsy stepped out, he leaned against it with all his weight. As he did so, he thought that this promised to be the worst storm he had ever encountered on the Atlantic crossing, and cursed silently because it could ruin all his plans to make this evening with Patsy the most memorable of all.

Due to the roll, he didn't see her step towards the companionway ahead. It led down to a short passage on the starboard side of the ballroom, where an orchestra still valiantly played for dancing. Officially, they performed there until midnight, then moved up to the Verandah Grill, but as yet it was barely eleven-thirty. Patsy called over her shoulder, "A few stalwarts are still dancing – or trying to!"

She turned, laughing, and it was then that the accident happened. A violent lurch caught her off balance and sent her hurtling down the companionway. She bounced from step to step like a helpless doll and by the time Colin reached the top she lay spreadeagled below.

Shocked, he saw that she lay with one leg twisted grotesquely beneath her. When he tried to pick her up she uttered a short sharp cry, and fainted.

CHAPTER TEN

WALKER's prediction that the surgery staff would be rushed off their feet if the storm broke proved only too true. Within minutes it began – the ceaseless ringing of the telephone, the harassed demands of cabin stewards and stewardesses, the urgent summonses from prostrate passengers declaring themselves at death's door, and the trail of minor accidents from the foolhardy who promenaded the deck just to prove to themselves, and others, what good sailors they were. Sprained ankles and bruised ribs, Sister Collard pointed out severely, were likely to be the fate of those unaccustomed to lurching decks. Doctored and subdued, they were only too willing to seek refuge in their bunks after that.

Maude had returned to duty the moment the storm broke, for which Lesley was thankful. Coping with the rush with only Walker's help would have been difficult. Mike took charge with brisk efficiency, sparing Lesley not a glance. He seemed aware of her only as a pair of hands to execute his commands. It was impossible to believe that only a short while ago she had experienced a passionate side of his nature – equally hard to believe that such a side existed, or that he had anything more than a coldly clinical mind.

They were doctor and nurse again, nothing more.

But for the first time she saw the humane side of him, the side both Sister Collard and Walker had vouched for, and which she had refused to credit. But as far as his patients were concerned, it was there. He was solicitous for their comfort and diligent in his attention; his touch was gentle and his sympathy sincere. Grudgingly, she granted him that.

Inevitably, Lady Travitt was amongst the most violent complainers, threatening to sue the Line for building an unseaworthy vessel and demanding the doctor's attention immediately. "And no one else's!" she shouted down the telephone.

Mike ordered, "Come with me, Nurse. She probably needs nothing more than a sleeping draught, or a shot in the arm."

He was right. Elvira moaned fretfully: "How is one expected to sleep in a hullabaloo like this? I thought modern vessels were built to withstand storms."

"Blame the elements, not the ship," Mike said. "You'd be worse off on a less luxurious one. At least, on the *Regina*, you can be ill in comfort!"

He signalled to Lesley to open her drug kit, and smiled down at the old lady with unexpected kindness.

Lesley placed her bag on a nearby table and opened it briskly, sending a framed photograph hurtling to the floor.

"Take care of that!" Elvira snapped. "Don't you dare damage Carol's picture!"

Lesley retrieved it quickly. Luckily, the thick carpet had prevented any breakage and she looked down into the smiling face of a striking young woman. There was both character and petulance in the features; determination in the chin and sensitivity in the mouth. An unusual face, and an interesting one. Was this the daughter Maude had talked about, the one who was on the stage in New York and married to an American producer?

And could it be the Carol to whom Walker had referred – the girl Mike had been going to marry?

Against her will, Lesley looked at the photograph again. The eyes were beautiful, the brow intelligent, the whole face very lovely.

She turned aside, busying herself with the sedative. There were hundreds of Carols in the world, but hadn't Elvira said something significant about the doctor and her daughter? " . . . not so quickly as he would have come when my daughter Carol was travelling with me—"

The old lady stretched out her bony hand and picked up the photograph, studying it with an odd mixture of pride and wistfulness. Then she held it towards Mike and said: "Good, isn't it? Carol's latest picture. Do you think she has changed much?"

Lesley stood waiting, glass in hand. Both the doctor and Lady Travitt appeared to have forgotten her. She was glad of that, for her heart was suddenly still.

"Go on, go on! Take a look at it, Mike. It shouldn't hurt you after all this time!"

So it *was* that Carol . . .

Mike took the photograph and studied it impassively, his face revealing no reaction whatsoever. Lesley felt a sudden sympathy with him. The old lady's taunt had been rather cruel, she thought.

"Drink up, Lady Travitt," she said with professional briskness, but her attempt to keep a note of disapproval from her voice must have failed, for the faded eyes darted to her in surprise, then brightened visibly. *You old tartar!* Lesley thought. *You're actually enjoying yourself!*

With deceptive meekness, Elvira drank. Mike had replaced the photograph and turned to the door.

"Well?" the woman rasped. "What *do* you think of her now?"

"She is as beautiful as ever, of course. I'll say good night now. Nurse Owen will settle you." He turned to

Lesley. "I have another patient to visit along this corridor. I shan't need you, so you can go straight back to the surgery."

The door closed behind him. Lesley adjusted the pillows, smoothed the sheets, rinsed the medicine glass and closed her drug case, and all the time she was aware of the old woman's eyes watching her. When at last she was forced to meet them, Elvira chuckled.

"I shocked you, didn't I, Nurse?"

"Yes. It was a cruel thing to do."

"Ah – so you've guessed he was in love with her, have you?"

"You made that fairly obvious, Lady Travitt."

"*As* I intended!"

Lesley switched off the light. In the darkness, the wrinkled hand caught hers.

"I had to do it – don't you understand? I had to make him look at her. It's about time he faced up to reality."

"Doctors face up to it more than most people." Lesley placed the hand beneath the sheet.

"You're angry with me, Nurse." The tone was hurt.

"Yes, I am, because what you did was embarrassing as well as cruel. Embarrassing for him, I mean. Didn't you realise that *I* was here – a member of his staff?"

"That was the reason I did it! I thought it would interest you to know that once upon a time he loved my daughter."

Lesley gasped.

"And why should it interest me?"

"You should know that better than I," the old lady answered drily.

Lesley marched to the door. As she opened it, a sleepy voice followed her from the bed.

"I said, Nurse, that he loved her – *once upon a time*—"

The storm was so high that Lesley had to cling to the handrail on her way back to the surgery. Her progress was therefore slow, and suddenly her arm was seized in a supporting clasp.

"Haven't found your sea legs yet, have you? Hang on to me."

It was Mike. His voice was impersonal, and she was as thankful for that as she was for his supporting arm.

"My other patient was asleep, thank goodness – his steward had given him something which apparently did the trick. Why do passengers demand the attention of Sick Bay for the most paltry ailments? Our chief steward has a highly experienced crew . . . "

A violent lurch thrust Lesley against him. He steadied her, then continued in the same impersonal vein, "The ship has slowed down several knots – can't you feel it? If this storm continues we'll be delayed. That means a quick turn around in New York. A pity. It won't leave you much time to see the sights, if that's what you're planning to do."

She hadn't made any plans at all. She had scarcely thought about New York or what would happen when they arrived there; not even how many hours they would be in port before sailing on to Florida. At the back of her mind had been some unformed idea that Colin would show her around, that they would spend all their time together, but he had not suggested anything yet. Time enough, she thought. Time enough.

They were nearing the surgery when Mike suddenly stood still and, holding Lesley by the elbows, turned her to face him.

"About what happened earlier this evening, I'd like to say—"

She jerked away.

"Please – forget it."

It was hard to be dignified when the world beneath her feet threatened to catapult her back into his arms. She reached blindly for the handrail and felt him grasp her shoulders again. To her surprise, he shook her impatiently.

"Listen to me, for God's sake. Don't you realise that I didn't mean it to happen?"

"You meant the things you said!" she retorted.

"All things spoken in the heat of the moment are meant, but only *for* that moment! But I apologised, and meant it."

If the ship would only stand still, she thought wildly, I could push him aside and stand on my own two feet! As it was, he had her at a disadvantage.

"I don't want to discuss it, Doctor."

"But *I* do." His grip tightened. "I want to discuss you and Colin Butler, also. As soon as this storm is over, I'd like to get the whole situation straight."

"What situation? And in what way does it concern you?"

He didn't answer that. Instead, he asked, "Is it true that you came on this ship because he was on it?"

"Why not? Why shouldn't a girl want to be near the man she is going to marry?"

It seemed somehow significant that, the moment she had spoken, there was a lull in the storm, as if the world outside was holding its breath. In the midst of the silence, Mike said tensely, "I've already apologised for the things I said; now I'd like you to know that I *don't* apologise for what I did, because I am no more sorry about it than you are. Remember that, when you're married to this man. Remember how you responded to one you hated, and ask yourself why."

She thrust him aside and turned blindly towards the surgery, but as she reached it, Mike's hand reached before her and opened the door. They entered the room together and saw a figure lying on the examination couch; a girl in a sparkling evening gown. It was Patsy, her face white and her eyes closed, and over her stooped the maternal figure of Sister Collard.

But it wasn't Maude at whom Lesley stared, nor Patsy, but Colin, whose head jerked up in relief. "Thank God, you've come, Doctor! Take a look at her quickly!"

Mike had already brushed him aside and replaced Maude beside the couch. His expert fingers were examining Patsy's leg, which Maude had already uncovered. He was brisk and professional again. "She has taken a bad fall. Down a companionway, I suppose?"

Colin could only stammer incoherently: "She's going to be all right, isn't she? She's – she's not—"

"She's not fatally injured, if that's what you're afraid of. Being rendered unconscious in falling doesn't necessarily mean anything more than slight concussion, but naturally we'll take a head X-ray to make sure, and we'll X-ray her leg as well, though I don't suspect anything more serious than a fractured tibia."

"You mean – she's broken her leg?"

"Below the knee. Painful, but by no means fatal. Prepare her for X-ray, will you, Nurse?"

Colin took a handkerchief from his pocket and wiped his brow in relief.

"Now leave us, will you, Butler? This place is too small for visitors. You can see the girl tomorrow, if Sister gives permission. And don't worry – she's in excellent hands. Nurse Owen will look after her."

Mike's eyes were on Lesley as he said that – his penetrating eyes which saw so much. As she wheeled Patsy from the room Lesley returned his glance. It was an effort, but she knew he was watching her and pride

144

made her lift her head. But, to her surprise, Mike's eyes were anything but cold. They were warm with compassion, but not for the patient. For herself. And that, if possible, was even more difficult to bear.

CHAPTER ELEVEN

As Mike had diagnosed, Patsy's injury was a straight-forward fracture. After setting, they strapped her on to a surgical trolley to brace her against the roll of the ship, and wheeled her to the admission bed Walker had prepared in Sick Bay.

Mike promised that as soon as the storm died down she could be transferred to her own quarters. "You'd prefer that, I'm sure, though you'll be comfortable here, and well looked after."

His smile was friendly and Patsy's, in return, grateful. She answered without thinking, "Well, that stateroom cost a pretty penny, so I'd like to get my money's worth!"

Mike laughed and patted her hand.

After settling the girl for the night, Lesley returned to the theatre. Setting a fracture was always a messy job, but because of the storm it had been even worse tonight. Plaster splashed the theatre floor as if a wild hand had thrown it. It was the first time Lesley had seen a fracture set in such conditions, and the doctor's skill impressed her.

The heaving theatre table had not only made the task more difficult, but had prolonged it. The time was now well past midnight. Lesley had been on duty since early morning, and fatigue touched her face with shadowy fingers. But her heart was heavy with more than tiredness.

Walker had already started to clean up, but there were routine tasks which Lesley had to attend to before going off duty. With mechanical precision she set about them, hardly aware, beneath her weariness, of what she did. She moved automatically, allowing her mind to run wherever it willed – which, inevitably, was to Colin. Anyone could see that he was distressed about Patsy, more distressed than was to be expected over a mere acquaintance.

The most galling thing was that Mike had seen it, too – and pitied her because of it. Of all things to endure, pity was the most humiliating, and, because it came from Mike, Lesley found it doubly so.

She started as his voice said, "You can leave these chores until morning, Nurse. There's nothing that can't wait until then."

"But there is. For one thing, the case book has to be brought up to date, and signed."

"I'll do both." He touched her shoulder briefly. "You've worked well, and I appreciate it. Don't look so surprised – I actually mean it."

There was a touch of humour in his voice which eased the tension between them.

"Run along," he said gently. "You look all in, poor child."

It was ridiculous to want to cry, but the sudden prick of tears behind her eyes made Lesley turn her head away quickly. The last thing she wanted to do was to break down in front of this man, but from the moment she had seen Colin's concern for Patsy she had felt alone and frightened. Now she wondered just how stubbornly, and for how long, a girl could blind herself to the obvious.

She walked out of the operating theatre like an automaton, shutting the door behind her. The case book was open on the surgery desk; she sat down and began to write, determined not to let the ship's doctor do her

147

work. She would show him that she was capable of carrying out her duties to the end.

She didn't glance up when the door opened again – not until a masculine hand reached in front of her and closed the book.

"I told you to go to bed. Didn't you hear me?"

"I am no more tired than you are."

"You're a damn sight more stubborn!"

"*That*," she declared, "would be impossible."

"All right!" he shouted. "Then perhaps you'll take notice of an *order*? A nurse swaying on her feet because of a storm is bad enough; I don't want her swaying through fatigue, as well. And goodness knows how long this gale will last – the forecast gives no hope of an early let-up. So now, you pig-headed young woman, will you do as you are told and *go to bed*?"

Her resistance subsided. She was suddenly unable to fight him any longer. She was even grateful to him, and said so.

"Thank you, Doctor. I would like to turn in, I admit."

What made her look back when she reached the door, she had no idea. He was standing there, watching her, and as their glances met an awareness of each other leapt between them. She stepped out into the corridor swiftly, closing the door behind her sharply.

To her surprise, she was face to face with Colin. He cried, "What an age you have been! Come and have a drink – you look all in."

"A drink – at this hour?"

"Why not? You look as if you could do with one, and I know I could. Licensing laws at sea aren't restricted like those ashore, thank heaven!"

There was a small cocktail lounge at the end of the corridor, with windows overlooking the deck. Colin propelled her towards it and seated her at a table. A tired steward served them, but Lesley sipped her drink without enthusiasm. She didn't want it, but she did want to talk to Colin.

She said without preliminary, "Patsy's going to be all right. It's a perfectly straightforward fracture with no complications. You'll be able to see her tomorrow." She smiled. "Today, I mean."

She didn't look at him. She didn't want to see the relief on his face. She wanted only one thing – to know the truth, and to know it right away, so before he could answer she blurted, "Are you in love with her, Colin?"

"Why do you ask that?" he jerked.

She took a long, hard look at him. She saw his handsome features and his well-shaped head and his very revealing eyes. She saw all the things which had always touched her heart and she viewed them quite dispassionately. He was as attractive as ever. Was it weariness, then, which made her react in a completely negative way?

"It seems a logical question," she said. "When we came into the surgery, the doctor and I, you were nearly frantic with anxiety."

"I don't know about frantic, but I was certainly anxious. Who wouldn't be? She had taken a header which could have killed her."

"Patsy's a healthy young woman, and healthy young women are amazingly tough. So are a lot of old ones! Look at Lady Travitt—"

"Oh – her," said Colin, as if he didn't even like the sound of her name.

"You still haven't answered my question. *Are* you in love with Patsy? Because, if so, I have a right to know."

He didn't answer immediately. He stared gloomily into his glass and she realised that he, too, was tired. Perhaps this wasn't the right moment for questions and explanations. Perhaps it would have been wiser to wait.

She finished her drink and said, "All right, Colin, don't answer now. It can wait. There'll be plenty of time before we dock. We'll be late reaching New York, thanks to the storm."

She half rose, but his hand detained her.

"No – I want to answer now. I want to tell you—"

But what Colin wanted to tell her she would never know, for at that moment she saw Mike staring at them from the open door, and the anger in his eyes froze her into immobility. It silenced Colin, too, who stared back without comment.

The doctor burst out furiously, "What the devil are you doing here, Nurse? I told you to turn in."

It seemed that they could never meet without sparks flying. Lesley felt an answering surge of anger and opened her mouth on a swift retort, but before she could utter it Mike continued furiously: "When I give an order I expect it to be obeyed – understand? I'll take insubordination from no one, Nurse Owen. *No one.* I suppose you imagine that being related to the company's chairman gives you the right to behave as you please?"

She had never seen him so angry, but his final words stunned her.

"A nurse who behaves as you do is no use to me. I'll recommend you for transfer to another vessel at the end of this trip. Better still, when we reach New York. Nothing would please me more than to off-load you onto another ship's doctor at the earliest opportunity."

CHAPTER TWELVE

As the storm continued and more passengers succumbed
to it, the medical unit was kept constantly busy. Lesley
was glad of this, for in work she could forget Mike
Halliday's injustice.

Patsy was a good patient. She was cheerful and un-
complaining, but gradually Lesley sensed something
beneath her stoicism – an emotional tension which, in
some odd way, seemed to be a direct reflection of her
own. Patsy was given to long and thoughtful silences.
She appeared to have something on her mind.

So had Lesley, who was aware that beneath her
resentment of Mike's attitude she was distressed at the
thought of failing him. To be dismissed by him was not
only humiliating, but proof that she had not succeeded
at her job. She should have obeyed him and refused to
allow herself to be sidetracked at the end of a long and
arduous day. She was well aware that the doctor was
within his rights to condemn her for disobedience, and
that the sight of her drinking with a male passenger in
the early hours of the morning was not one to recommend
her as a nurse. Of course, the fact that the man was
Colin had nothing to do with Mike's reaction; she was
sure of that.

All the same, he *had* been unjust, and pride made her
refuse to ask forgiveness. Nor had she the slightest in-
tention of explaining the situation, so from the moment
they came on duty again next morning they were frigid

and distant with each other, speaking only when work demanded.

And then something happened which, to Lesley, was very significant.

Some flowers came to the ward for Patsy, just before noon, and Lesley was there when they arrived; fresh flowers from the ship's florist, which transported supplies across the Atlantic in its own refrigeration unit so that any one placing an order at any time during the voyage could be supplied immediately. When Patsy took the accompanying card from its small gilt-edged envelope, a deep colour flooded her face.

Why Lesley was so certain that the gift came from Colin, she really had no idea, but the conviction was sharp.

She said automatically, "I'll fetch a vase—" but Patsy answered, "It's a shoulder spray. I suppose Colin chose it because a vase would be useless in a storm like this. How thoughtful of him!" She lifted the small sheaf from its wrappings and sniffed appreciatively. "Wearing flowers in bed will be another new experience for me!"

"A new experience? I should have thought there were few you had missed!"

"Why? Do I appear so blasée?"

"By no means. Merely rich enough to indulge most whims."

Patsy answered negligently, "Do you think so?" and did not speak again until Lesley returned with a pin and fixed the spray on her bed jacket.

"Nurse—"

"Yes, Miss Davis?"

"I do wish you'd call me Patsy! Everyone does."

Lesley smiled.

"Patsy, then. I must say I like it better."

They were very much at ease with each other. In other

circumstances they would probably have become firm friends, but there was a gulf between the ship's nurse and an exclusive passenger. Besides, there was something else, and that something else, though Patsy didn't realise it, was Colin.

"You were going to ask me something," Lesley reminded her. "What was it?"

"Just this. Does everyone think as you do – that I'm rich?"

"I imagine so. One just naturally concludes that anyone travelling as you are travelling on a ship like the *Regina* must be well able to afford it. Although if anyone should know differently, I should."

"What do you mean?"

"That I once travelled in state myself, and I don't suppose anyone suspected that it was by courtesy of my uncle!" (Even Colin had not guessed, she recalled with a pang.)

"Who is your uncle?"

"Chairman of the Line."

"My goodness, and you a ship's nurse!"

"Why not?"

"Appearances *are* deceptive, aren't they?"

Before Lesley could pursue the point, Colin followed up his gift with a personal visit which was to prove the first of many. His pleasure at seeing his flowers on Patsy's shoulder was self-evident.

"Don't I look grand?" she laughed. "All dressed for the ball! Colin, it was sweet of you to send them – and to come to see me."

"Did you think I'd stay away?"

She held out her hands spontaneously, and he took them in his own, and kept them there. Lesley quietly drew up a chair, placed it beside the bed, and left them. They didn't even notice her departure.

Outside, Sister Collard nodded her grey head towards the closed door.

"Got it badly, haven't they? I wonder if anything will come of it, or if it will turn out to be just another shipboard affair? If it does, I'll be disappointed. They seem well suited, those two."

Lesley answered thoughtfully, "I'm pretty sure something will come of it, Sister."

Maude looked at her junior nurse, recalling old Lady Travitt's information about her – that she had come abroad the *Regina* to be near that handsome young man now sitting devotedly beside Patsy Davis's bed. She had refused to believe it at the time, but something in Lesley's voice now made her wonder.

She asked carefully, watching Lesley's face, "It would be very romantic, wouldn't it, Nurse?" But the girl's face remained the calm inscrutable face of the well-trained nurse. Only her voice faltered a little as she answered, "Very romantic indeed, Sister."

Mike entered at that moment and conversation turned to medical matters. A few minutes later Sister said briskly, "It's time you dismissed the visitor, Nurse. Your patient will become too excited if he stays much longer."

"What visitor?" Mike asked, as Lesley crossed to the ward.

Maude glanced towards the door, saw that Lesley was out of earshot, and said, "A very attentive young man, Doctor – as you probably noticed last night. He seemed beside himself with anxiety."

Mike said nothing, and when Colin emerged a moment later the doctor appeared not to notice him.

Colin halted. "I'd like a word with you," he said.

"If it's about the patient, Nurse or Sister will report on her."

"It's not about the patient."

Maude withdrew tactfully, leaving the two men alone.

"Well?" the doctor asked.

"It's about Lesley — Nurse Owen. It was my fault — last night, I mean. I waited for her and persuaded her to have a drink with me."

"I imagine little persuasion was needed."

"In view of the weather, and one thing and another, we hadn't had a chance to talk. I was anxious to."

"I can appreciate that."

"You can?" Colin echoed, surprised.

"Naturally. Nurse Owen told me about your engagement—"

"Oh — that. She took it rather badly, I'm afraid."

For the first time, he had Mike's full attention.

"Took what badly?"

"My breaking it off."

Mike stared, then said levelly, "Is that what you were doing last night? Was that why you waited for her? Good grief, man, you might have had a little more consideration after the exhausting day she'd had!"

"Nothing of the sort! I broke it before she ever came aboard. In fact, that was *why* she came aboard."

"In that case, all I can say is that she must be pretty desperately in love with you."

"That's the damnable part—"

The intervening door reopened and Lesley appeared. Colin said swiftly, "I'm glad Miss Davis is going along all right, Doctor, and thanks for all you did for her." Then he was gone. Mike decided that young Butler could evade a situation more decisively than anyone he knew.

Doctor and nurse looked at one another. She met his penetrating glance; it seemed to look right through her. And he met a proud and stubborn young face which he wanted to take between his hands and kiss very gently. He was angry with her, but touched by her. He wanted to be with her, and yet to get away from her. He condemned her lack of pride and at the same time wondered why a girl like her could waste her love upon a man like Colin Butler, who didn't even deserve it.

The moment was disturbing and Lesley jerked away from it. She had enough on her mind just now without adding to it. Colin and Patsy had been sitting hand in hand when she entered the ward, and his glance, when meeting her own, had been one of guilt and discomfort. She had never seen Colin look like that before.

She was glad when the surgery door opened and Walker staggered in.

"Blimey, this storm don't get no better, does it? More than half the passengers are laid up, chief steward tells me, and the dining room's practically empty. We're going to be well behind schedule, aren't we, sir?"

Mike agreed, then, seeing Lesley heading for the door, asked where she was off to.

"To get my patient's lunch," she answered, and closed the door behind her. There was a new quality in Mike's glance which she didn't quite know how to meet; a glance of enquiry strangely mixed with compassion. What an inconsistent, illogical, *infuriating* man he was!

He was absent when she returned, and Patsy, propped up with pillows, was gazing at the swaying ceiling with a strange mixture of wistfulness and joy. Her expression changed to one of admiration as she watched Lesley's approach.

"How you manage to carry that tray without spilling anything, I just don't know!"

"Frankly, nor do I! I'm getting my sea legs, I suppose."

"Stay and talk to me, Nurse. Unless you're going for lunch yourself?"

"I have to wait until Sister returns. One of us must always be on duty."

Patsy surveyed the tray with frank appreciation.

"Remember how ill I was the first day out, and the weather absolutely calm compared with this? Now I feel wonderful, apart from my leg. Oh, please, Lesley – don't go!"

Reluctantly, Lesley lingered. She liked Patsy, but shunned a tête-à-tête with her. Automatically, she insisted that she should rest after eating her lunch.

"I will, I promise. At any rate, until Colin comes—"

"Are you expecting him again this afternoon?"

Patsy's glance was one of almost naïve anxiety.

"He may come, mayn't he? I mean, there aren't any rules and regulations about visiting hours, as in a hospital, are there?"

"Since you're alone in this ward, and not really ill, I don't imagine so."

There was a brief silence; a companionable silence on Patsy's part, but an uncomfortable one on Lesley's. She wanted to ask a question and couldn't. Coming from the ship's nurse it would appear unseemly, and without a suitable opening from Patsy, it was impossible anyway.

Patsy presented the opening quite suddenly.

"Have you ever been in love?" she asked breathlessly. "Don't think me crazy, but I simply must talk to someone or *die!*"

Lesley forced herself to say in her most professional voice, "My patients never die, Patsy, so I can't allow you to. Eat up that lunch!"

But the girl dropped her knife and fork on her plate, and forgot them.

"Help me," she begged. "Please help me!"

Lesley asked in surprise, "In what way?"

"Tell me what to do!" Patsy's hand reached out and

caught hers. "I can't lie here worrying any longer. I've got to confide in someone, or bust! And you're the most sympathetic person I've met on this ship—"

"I thought Colin was."

"But it's *about* him – so I can't *talk* to him! And it's about me, too, and that's the terribly important part."

Lesley wanted to escape. She wanted to hear no confidences about these two. "Patsy, don't say anything you might regret later."

"I won't regret it. All I'm likely to regret is keeping quiet in the first place. In fact, I regret that already. But I didn't think anything was likely to happen – oh, don't misunderstand! I don't mean that we've done anything wrong; only that I've been crazy enough to fall in love. But you've guessed that, I suppose?"

"Yes, I think I have."

"And the awful thing is that I'm afraid he's in love with me!"

"You're – sure of that?"

Patsy nodded her bright head emphatically. "Certain-sure. Just as I'm sure that if I owned up, he'd drop me at once."

"Owned up about what? I don't understand."

"That I'm not what I seem. Not what he thinks me."

"You mean you're married, or something?"

"Oh, no. Much worse than that."

Lesley couldn't help laughing. "My dear Patsy, what could be worse?"

"I mean that the deception I've practised is worse. I knew why he was running after me – at least, I suspected it in the first place and then, one night in the smoking-room, I asked him point blank if he thought money was all that important. I even asked if he planned to marry for it. Why shouldn't I ask questions if I want to know the answers? And the answer was important."

Lesley asked tautly, "What did he say?"

"Nothing. He evaded it. So that told me a lot. And so I went right on pretending, because I'd gone too far to stop."

Lesley stared. "Patsy – are you trying to tell me—?"

" – that I'm as poor as the proverbial church mouse? Yes. Or will be when I get back home again."

"I don't believe it!"

"You said yourself that no one would have believed *you* weren't rich when you 'travelled in state'. The difference between us is that I did pay for my own trip, but I won't have a bean left at the end of it. Don't look so astonished. It's perfectly simple. I won five thousand pounds in a beauty queen competition – Miss E.E.C. The first ever. Looks make up the only commodity I've been generously endowed with, and they don't last for ever. Nor did my prize money. I've never had a taste of real luxury in my life, or excitement. Just a bed-sit in Dulwich and second-hand romance from the library."

Impulsively, Lesley's arms went round the girl. Against her shoulder, Patsy whispered: "So now you understand why I didn't tell Colin. Being what he is, he'd drop me like a hot brick if he knew the truth."

Lesley was silent. For the first time, she let the blinkers slip from her eyes. Patsy had courage enough to acknowledge facts when she saw them – but I, Lesley thought bitterly, went on deluding myself even when the evidence was thrust upon me.

"You know Colin, don't you, Lesley? Have you known him long?"

"Fairly."

"And well?"

"Yes. Very well."

"Has he always been ambitious; over-ambitious, I mean, valuing people solely for their money?"

"Not solely for it, Patsy. Not *solely* for it, I'm sure."

"Well," said Patsy practically, "*I'm* not sure, and until I am, I'm saying nothing. Anyway, it's too late now. I'm up to my ears in love with him."

"So he is with you," Lesley replied seriously.

"Ah, but will he remain so, if he finds out the truth? I doubt it. I can read him like a book. I know all his faults and his weaknesses."

"And love him in spite of them?"

Patsy answered simply, "Love doesn't demand perfection."

But *I* did, Lesley thought. I had my own idea of Colin; I put my own interpretation on his character, and I couldn't love anything less. But this girl can, and does, because *she* really loves him – and I didn't. I loved only the picture I had of him . . .

"You're looking very pensive," Patsy remarked. "A penny for them."

"You can have them for nothing! I was thinking that I've never really been in love before."

"Before? Does that mean you are now?"

But Lesley merely smiled and answered briskly, "If you've finished that lunch, it's time for your rest. And no worrying, mind." Spontaneously, she dropped a kiss on the girl's cheek. "You're just about the nicest person I've ever met, Patsy Davis, and if Colin gets you, he'll be lucky."

It was amazing how light-hearted she felt as she left the ward, how oblivious of everything but her own sense of release. It was even more than that. It was a feeling of discovery, too, and because she, like Patsy, wanted to face facts, she was glad to find the surgery empty. It was important to be alone.

She faced the facts fairly and squarely. Elvira Travitt had been right about Colin, and now Patsy was right about him, too. But, unlike Elvira, the girl didn't condemn his faults. She was right in saying that love didn't demand perfection.

Lesley admitted frankly to herself that she could never love Colin that way. She was disillusioned, not touched, by his true character. She saw him as a different person, and one who no longer meant anything to her. Love could not change overnight, just like that, surely? Not unless something deeper and stronger and more real had taken its place . . .

She faced that fact squarely, too. Something had. Something which had come to life the moment Mike Halliday's lips touched her own – even before, perhaps, when emotion had sparked between them like a threatening fire. It had kindled at their first moment of meeting and had smouldered ever since. And she had called it hatred.

She covered her face with her hands, feeling again the torrent of emotion his passion had stirred in her; feeling the strength of his arms and her own surrender. Forthright, hot-tempered, and unjust he might be, but despite those qualities she wanted to go on working for him, simply because she wanted to be near him for ever. If that wasn't love, what was?

The irony of it stabbed her to the heart. After making an enemy of the man right from the beginning of the voyage; after getting on the wrong side of him on every possible occasion, she discovered now, when it was too late, that she had fallen hopelessly and irrevocably in love with him. And, this time, it was the real thing.

CHAPTER THIRTEEN

BEING confined to her bed put no brake on Lady Travitt's curiosity; she was as eager as ever to keep in touch with shipboard life, and said so.

"Don't think that because I'm out of circulation, Sister, I'm tucked quietly out of the way! That's why I've sent for you. I want a full report of everything that's going on."

Maude Collard answered crisply, "Seventy-five per cent of the passengers are sea-sick, twenty per cent are pretending not to be, and the remaining five per cent are just plain bored. A sea voyage in conditions like this is tedious even to the most hardened sailor. There – now you have your report. What else do you want?"

"Nurse Owen. In fact, I hoped *she* would answer my summons."

"At the beginning of the voyage you declared you wouldn't be attended by her whatever happened."

"That," Elvira retorted crisply, "was at the beginning of the voyage."

"Well, she's busy right now. She has a patient to look after in Sick Bay, and duties elsewhere besides."

"You're keeping her away from me deliberately. Don't think I can't guess why."

"Then tell me, for *I* can't guess why, I assure you."

"It's because you know perfectly well that I'm interested in her and you're afraid I'll start questioning her."

"And so you would."

Lady Travitt smiled wickedly.

"Of course I would. I'd have to, wouldn't I, stuck here in my bed and unable to know what's going on?"

"Nothing *is* going on, except in Sick Bay, where we are rushed off our feet."

"Who's the resident patient down there?"

"A passenger."

The old woman looked at Sister's impassive face and snapped, "You think you're clever, don't you? You think that doesn't tell me anything? Well, I'm sorry to disappoint you, but I *know* who the patient is."

"Then why ask?"

Maude looked at the wizened old face, at the dyed hair swathed in tulle, at the shrunken shoulders bedecked with a fluffy bed jacket more suited to the glamorous little Patsy Davis, and felt a not unfamiliar pity.

"It's the girl next door, isn't it, Sister? I heard about her accident from the stewardess. I might say I get a great deal more attention since that attractive little minx moved out."

"She'll be moving back just as soon as it's calm enough to transport her without difficulty. Not that she isn't comfortable enough in Sick Bay, but I'm sure she'd prefer to be in her own quarters."

"Tell me—" Elvira's eyes were agog. "Is she having any visitors?"

Maude was spared the trouble of answering that question by the unexpected arrival of Mike, who knocked briefly on the door and, when summoned, filled the aperture with his size. Not for the first time Sister Collard noticed what a strong figure of a man he was.

"I came to see how you were, Elvira. Walker told me you'd been ringing."

"Sister came along," Lady Travitt answered unnecessarily, and Maude moved to the door.

"She's doing fine, Doctor. The minute the storm begins to lull it would do her good to get up on deck again."

"It would do a lot of people good to get up on deck again," he agreed, and smiled at Maude as she departed.

"Well, Mike? To what do I owe the honour of this unexpected call? Don't try to pretend you were concerned for my welfare, because I know perfectly well, from the stewardess, that you've been rushed off your feet, so I don't suppose you've even thought about *me*."

He answered tolerantly, "I don't have to declare that I'm concerned for your welfare, Elvira, because you know perfectly well that I am. However, I knew that either Sister Collard or Nurse Owen would be keeping an eye on you, and that you would understand if I didn't."

"Then why are you here? Not that I'm not glad to see you. I like you, Mike Halliday. I always have and I always will. Carol was a fool."

"Let's leave Carol out of this, shall we?"

"That's rather difficult because I had a cable from her today, asking if you were on board. She wants to see you again. She's coming to meet me at New York. If you don't want to see her, you needn't, but I think it would be a good idea if you did."

She didn't say why. She merely observed the slight frown which touched Mike's brow, and wished she could interpret it. He was a difficult man to read, a hard man to understand – but it was a pity there weren't a few more like him in the world, all the same.

For a moment he was silent. The mention of Carol had intruded into his life at a time when he least welcomed it. His thoughts were too deeply involved with Lesley and Colin Butler. It was obvious that the girl was still in love with him.

The whole situation troubled Mike – he couldn't get

Lesley out of his mind. What insane impulse had prompted him to kiss her, and what mysterious alchemy had made him so strongly aware of her all along?

And now Carol threatened to come back into his life again. The realisation that he could regard this as merely tiresome was startling. He had loved her for so long that if anyone had told him he could ever love another woman he would have denied it emphatically. Yet now he was not so sure . . .

Being unsure of anything was a new experience to a man like Mike Halliday.

"Well?" Elvira demanded, watching him carefully. "You don't look too pleased. Don't you want to see Carol?"

"To be honest, I don't mind one way or the other," he answered unexpectedly, and the truth of this statement startled him even further. But not Elvira, who merely nodded her head in satisfaction.

"I thought you wouldn't, dear boy. And do you know why?"

He didn't want to know why – at least, not from her. Not from anyone but himself, and not until he was absolutely alone. There would be time enough to face the truth then.

"I came to talk to you about Patsy Davis," he said. "We've made a mistake, you and I, in hiding things."

"You think so?" The old lady's voice was non-committal, even wary, but Mike was too absorbed to notice.

"We've let things go too far, Elvira. She's fallen in love with Butler and you know what that means – she's going to be hurt."

"You think so?" the old lady said again.

"It's obvious. Butler's an ambitious type."

"Aren't you overlooking something – the reason for our keeping silent? It was for the benefit of your nurse, not Patsy Davis."

"They're both going to be hurt."

"Every woman is, at some time or another. It's better for them to experience it when young. They grow into more mature women as a result. Softer. Kinder. More understanding. Marry a woman who's been disappointed in love, Mike, and she'll make you happy. She will appreciate you and love you all the better because of it. Carol could never love you that way because she has never cared enough about any man to be really hurt by him, and if you think that a strange admission for a woman to make about her own daughter – well – maybe you're right."

"It is an honest admission," he answered gently, but you are the most honest woman I know."

"You loved Carol deeply, didn't you?"

"Yes. I did."

"I hope you haven't let it embitter you for ever? It did for a time, I know, but that wouldn't be fair to the girl you will eventually marry."

"I doubt if I shall ever marry."

Elvira checked a knowing smile.

"But you will meet Carol when she comes aboard, won't you? They're sure to let her come aboard to greet me. They always do."

"Of course I'll meet her."

"Her divorce should be through quite soon – they're very speedy about these things in America. But she will tell you all about it herself, I'm sure. It may even be her true reason for coming to meet the ship, knowing you are on it," Elvira finished with a touch of sadness.

Mike covered her hand with his.

"Don't think, or say, things like that. Carol's love for

you is evident in her need of you. Even though she has always gone her own way, she has kept in constant touch, hasn't she? Other people have been tossed by the way-side, but not her mother. She turns to you in every moment of need, and in between as well, and believe me, my dear, she always will. Because you understand her better than anyone, and she knows it, and you're the one person in the world she cannot do without."

The old woman's tired eyes lit up.

"I do believe you're right," she whispered.

"I know I am," he answered briskly, "just as I know I was wrong to agree to your outrageous scheme to hide the truth about Patsy Davis from Colin Butler. If that girl is hurt, I shan't forgive myself – or you, you scheming old lady."

"And what about your nurse? Isn't she likely to be hurt if we don't let her see that young man in his true colours? That *was* our main object, remember."

"I think she has been hurt already," Mike answered slowly.

"And what makes you think that?"

"I don't know ... "

And he didn't. Lesley's thoughts and emotions were anything but an open book to him. He was bewildered for the first time in his life; bewildered by her passionate response to his kisses, when all the time believing herself in love with another man, a man she was so determined to marry that she had come aboard the *Regina* especially to be near him.

A question leapt into his mind. Why had it been necessary for her to go about it in such an extraordinary way? In view of who she was, couldn't she have booked a passage as a normal passenger and rivalled Patsy Davis on her own ground?

The thought so absorbed him that he scarcely heard

Elvira's next words, and it wasn't until she repeated them that he jerked to attention.

"Well, Mike, what do you propose to do? Break the news to Butler about Patsy's real circumstances?"

"No. I imagine the girl wants to keep silent about it, otherwise she would have told him already."

"And you're quite sure she hasn't?"

"My instinct tells me not. But it's more than instinct really – it's the fact that he's been visiting her regularly in Sick Bay and if he knew the truth about her, I imagine he wouldn't bother."

"And how has that nice nurse reacted to his visits?"

"I have no idea."

That was true enough. Lesley presented an unrevealing front to everyone. Not for the world would she let anyone pry into the deep corners of her heart, for the truth she had discovered about herself was too precious and too important to be revealed. She knew perfectly well that Mike would never love her, but that didn't stop her from nursing her secret with a kind of wonder and enchantment which imparted a subtle change to her whole personality.

Even Mike was aware of it when he returned to the surgery. She met him without any resentment, even though their last meeting had been a painful and memorable one. His dismissal of her had been abrupt and without thought; a blind attack prompted by his own jealousy.

But he was too proud to climb down, or even seek a truce. He knew she wouldn't want it, anyway.

He was right. Lesley's manner was polite, professional, and absolutely impersonal. There was no indication that she even remembered their last meeting, and certainly no suggestion of pique. She was the crisp and efficient nurse again, which only served to increase Mike's awareness of how little he mattered to her. She was apparently quite unperturbed at the thought of leaving the *Regina*.

They discussed work amicably for some time, then Lesley said, "Is it my imagination, or is the storm really less violent?"

"It's not your imagination. It's getting quieter."

"Then perhaps my patient can be transferred to her room? She would like that, I'm sure."

"And you?" he asked unexpectedly. "Would you like that, too?"

"As her nurse, I would naturally prefer her to remain in Sick Bay. She would be under my eye constantly then – it's a long walk to her stateroom."

"I didn't mean that. I meant that if she were out of the way you wouldn't be hurt by Butler's constant visits to her."

Lesley made no answer, and Mike experienced a sudden urge to make her face the truth. He wanted to thrust it before her, no matter how painful it was. This girl was now thoroughly under his skin and nothing he did could get her out of his thoughts. That was enough to goad any man.

"Well?" he demanded. "Don't pretend you haven't been aware of his anxiety for her, and his ever-hovering presence."

"I don't pretend. I'd have been a fool, and blind, not to see both."

"Well, then?"

"I don't see that it has anything to do with either you or me. We are merely her doctor and nurse."

He gave her a long, penetrating glance, before which she turned away.

"Look at me," he ordered.

Dutifully, she obeyed.

"Did you, or did you not, tell me you were engaged to this man?"

"I was engaged to him, yes."

There was a barely perceptible emphasis on the past tense.

"Even the other night, when I dismissed you?"

"I believed so."

"And now?"

"Now I realise he doesn't love me. Perhaps he never did."

He said gently, "I'm sorry, Lesley – believe me. I wouldn't want you to be hurt."

The softness of his voice was so disturbing that she turned away from it, saying briskly, "And I don't want Patsy to be hurt. I feel I ought to do something to prevent it, and I just don't know what."

"Why should she be hurt?" he asked carefully.

"Because if Colin knew the truth about her, he would do to her what he did to me. I may as well own up. Colin tried to break our engagement before the *Regina* sailed, and I – well, I just couldn't believe it. I think perhaps that was why my uncle helped me to get this job. Maybe he saw through Colin and wanted me to do the same."

Mike glanced at his watch.

"Four o'clock. We can knock off for a cup of tea, and I think it would be a good idea if you told me everything – *everything*, mark you – whilst we have it. There are a number of things I don't understand."

Giving her no chance to answer he took hold of her elbow and led her from the surgery to his own sitting room, where he rang for tea and then said, "We can talk here undisturbed. From the beginning, please – the very beginning. I think you ought to know that Butler recently told me about breaking your engagement."

Even that didn't seem to disturb her.

"Then it saves me the trouble of giving you details."

"I'd like to hear them, all the same, and I don't care if you think I have no right to ask."

"I am perfectly sure that if you wanted to find out something, you would ask, whether you had the right to, or not."

"Perfectly true," he admitted blandly. "Now go ahead and tell me everything."

"There's little to tell, really. Colin broke our engagement, and I wouldn't accept it, so I applied for a job on this ship."

"In order to be near him."

"Partly. But there was another motive. I wanted to prove to him that I could work – *and* hold down a job. He didn't believe me capable of either." She smiled, wryly. "And after the way you dismissed me the other night, he won't believe it now!" Not that it mattered, she thought with a sense of relief. The burden of proving herself to Colin had been removed, and she was thankful for it.

"I'm sorry," Mike said, "but what I don't understand is *why* you had to prove it."

She explained patiently, "Because we couldn't get married otherwise. We couldn't afford to."

"But he has a good job. And besides—"

"Besides," she finished drily, "I am supposed to have money, aren't I? Remember what you called me when I first came aboard? You thought I was an idle-rich girl, playing at working."

He had the grace to look embarrassed. She had longed for such a moment as this, ever since they met, but it gave her little satisfaction, after all. She said swiftly: "I don't blame you, any more than I blame Colin for believing my father was wealthy. I was as surprised as

171

he when I learned the truth. My father died, you see, and it wasn't until then that it all came out. Father didn't leave a penny, but oddly enough I was glad of that. I thought Colin would be, too. I thought he would welcome the idea of standing on our own feet, of working for our home together . . . "

It was surprising how easy it was to talk about things – and to this man, of all people. She had resolved that on no account should Doctor Halliday ever know the truth about her, yet here she was, laying it all before him.

The arrival of tea interrupted the conversation, and when the steward had withdrawn Mike said, "Go on."

"There's nothing more, really. Colin felt he couldn't support me 'at the standard to which I was accustomed' and decided he was standing in my way. At least, that's what he said, and I believed it. So I wanted to prove him wrong. I wanted to show him that *I* was capable of working for our home, too."

"You must love him very much," Mike said quietly.

A shutter seemed to come down between them. She refused to admit that in recognising the truth about Colin she had been cured of her infatuation, because that might also reveal a further truth which, at all costs, she was determined to keep to herself.

"You said just now," Mike continued briskly, "that you didn't want Patsy to be hurt. What makes you think she will be?"

"Because she is right about him – Colin, I mean. If he knew that she, too—" She broke off, biting her full lower lip.

" – that she, too, has no money?" Mike finished. "You are not the only one to have learned the truth about Patsy. Lady Travitt and I have known for a long time, but decided to keep silent."

"For Patsy's sake? But why?"

"Not merely for Patsy's sake." He continued quickly, "You said just now that she was right about him. Do you mean that she's seen through him?"

"She sees him just as he is – and loves him just the same. That's why I'm afraid she is going to be hurt. And I simply don't know what to do to help her!"

"Only one person can help Patsy, and that's herself. If she's sensible enough to face up to the truth about him, as she appears to have done without anybody's aid, she is courageous enough to face him with the truth about herself."

It was time to return to duty. The tension between them had eased to such an extent that Lesley suddenly heard herself asking if he would revise his decision to dismiss her.

He raised his eyebrows mockingly. "Sack the niece of the Company's chairman? My dear girl, a mere ship's doctor can't do that. All I can do is pass you on to burden the life of another unfortunate man."

"Then I can only describe my release as a happy one. Believe me, working for such a man as you has equipped me for enduring something far worse than a mere Atlantic gale!"

He gave a shout of laughter and Lesley found herself joining in, and so they stood there, laughing together, and in that moment something tremulous and lovely finally came to life, something which united them in happiness and expectancy. He caught both her hands in his and, laughing down at her, said frankly, "Be that as it may, I can assure you of this – that not at any price would I have you as my ship's nurse again!"

She looked at him – bewildered, questioning, not knowing if he were serious, not knowing how to interpret his remark at all. Would she ever understand this man, or ever get to know him?

The storm died down as rapidly as it had risen. Patsy was wheeled back to her stateroom, fortified by the assurance that once the sea was really calm again she could be dressed and taken up on deck.

"I'll tell Colin. I'm sure he would like to take you there. You can prop up that plastered leg in a deck chair and inhale the sea air."

Patsy caught hold of Lesley's hand. "I don't want to be left alone with him, not for a minute! Please, promise you'll see that I'm not!"

"But I have work to do – I'm not on this ship for a pleasure cruise, Patsy. Besides, you can't have someone with you all the time. You're bound to be alone with him eventually."

"I don't see why. We'll be late reaching New York, even if the ship goes full speed ahead from now on. Between now and the time we dock there are hours to kill. And I don't want to spend any of them alone with Colin."

"Patsy—"

"No – I mean it. Don't try to dissuade me! I'll say goodbye to him when we dock and after that I'll never see him again. It's better that way."

"He may not agree. He may be determined to see you."

"I'm sailing straight back. Purser's office is arranging it for me. There's another ship sailing out of New York within a couple of days. We'll be there in time for me to be transferred. That will be much better than being laid up, incapacitated, in some strange hotel – and hiding from Colin."

"You are quite determined not to see him again?"

"Quite."

It was no use trying to dissuade her. And perhaps, thought Lesley, her decision was the wisest after all.

Within an hour of the first lull, the storm was over, the seas were calm again, and the ship came to life once more. The old familiar "regulars" emerged on deck; pallid faces lay back on deck chairs, gradually regaining their normal colour. People even began to think about food. Later that evening, the dining room began to fill up again and the dance orchestra took its place in the ballroom.

Lesley, in a brief off-duty spell, helped Patsy to dress. A full length gown of gold organza hid her leg in its plaster cast, and but for sticks and a lumbering gait she looked little the worse for her accident. The ship's hairdresser sent an assistant to her stateroom and when she emerged for dinner she looked as lovely as before. Lesley helped her to the lift, which carried them down to the restaurant.

Colin was waiting at the table he shared with Patsy, and his eyes, as Lesley brought the girl towards him, were self-revealing. She left him to instal Patsy in her chair, and went to join Maude at their own table.

"Well, my dear?" Maude asked briskly. "Are you too tired, after these hectic days, to give me a hand with that dress?"

"I'd like to, very much."

"Tomorrow?"

"Tonight, if you like. After dinner."

"Nonsense, child. That's your off-duty time, and you've earned it."

"Which gives me the right to do what I like with it. I'll come along to your cabin."

"Bless you. I'll have a sewing machine sent along there. I'd love to have that dress ready to wear in New York."

"I don't see why you shouldn't. Did you manage to get those seams tacked before the storm began?"

"Only just! But they're ready."

"Then it's merely a question of fitting and machining and pressing. I'm sure we can do it."

Lesley was glad to have the prospect of some occupation, for now her off-duty hours spread ahead of her, empty and idle. There would be no more secret meetings with Colin on deck. If she had any further time alone with him, it would be to say goodbye. The prospect of parting with him left her curiously indifferent. It was odd that after being so important in her life he should suddenly matter so little, whereas the thought of parting from Mike was unbearable.

She ate little, and soon left Maude on the pretext of seeing Patsy back to bed. "I don't want her tiring herself out, first time up," she said, and found to her surprise that Patsy was only too willing to retire. She was quiet and unusually depressed.

Preparing for bed with one leg in a plaster cast proved a troublesome business. Patsy was glad of Lesley's help, and reluctant to part with her company.

"I hope you didn't have coffee at your table," she said, "because I'd be glad if you would have some here with me."

"I was planning to have it on deck before going below to help Sister Collard with some dressmaking."

"But not yet!" Patsy's tone was urgent. "Colin is coming, so I've ordered for three. Don't forget that I begged you not to leave me alone with him."

Reluctantly, Lesley was forced to agree. When Colin arrived, Patsy was lying on a couch, her ungainly plaster cast hidden by a flowered house coat.

There was a slight strain in the atmosphere, but mainly on Colin's side. Patsy's chatter was tinged with a kind of desperate gaiety. Only Lesley was really calm and untroubled. Colin seemed uneasy, less self-confident than usual. Was he aware of Patsy's determination not to be alone with him again, Lesley wondered, and just how greatly did he mind? Pretty much, judging by his efforts to please her.

These efforts were not lost on Patsy, either. Throughout dinner she had spoken little, finding conversation with him too great a strain. It was easy to pretend that her accident had left her feeling tired and weak; it served as an excuse to cover a reluctance to talk, but she could not continue like that indefinitely, and the sooner she put an end to all pretence, the better.

She poured the coffee, handing Lesley's cup to Colin to pass on. As he accepted it, Lesley was surprised to notice that his hand trembled slightly.

Conversation was desultory – idle comments about the storm, and the delayed arrival in New York, and the ship's efforts to catch up on time. The distant throb of the engines came to them with a remote kind of urgency.

"Personally," announced Patsy, "I don't mind how late we arrive, but I expect it matters a lot to people like yourself, Colin."

"I have appointments, of course." He spoke absent-mindedly, stirring his coffee and not looking at either of them. "But people usually understand these things. Storms have delayed transatlantic liners before."

"What will you do when you get back to England at the end of the cruise?" Patsy asked Lesley. "Get ready for the next one?"

"No. I'll be looking for another job, or transferring to another vessel. Possibly even at New York."

"You didn't tell me!"

"I didn't know myself, until the other night. But Colin did. He was there when Doctor Halliday dismissed me."

"He *what*?"

Colin put in, "He didn't exactly dismiss you, Lesley. He merely said he would arrange for your transfer to another ship."

"And what is that, but the sack in fancy dress?"

Patsy cried, "It's outrageous! More than that, it's extraordinary. I could have sworn that doctor was in love with you!"

Lesley's coffee spoon rattled in its saucer. She laughed, but not very successfully.

"My dear Patsy, what an imagination you have! Doctor Halliday has never even liked me."

"That I *know* to be untrue! I've seen him looking at you when you have been quite unaware of it. I didn't waste my time, down in Sick Bay, I can tell you. There was little to do but watch the comings and goings of the medical staff, or lie in bed, thinking about my own affairs. And I didn't enjoy doing that very much . . . "

"Why not?" Colin asked.

"Because my own affairs aren't very pleasant to think about, right now."

She checked an impulse to hold out a beseeching hand to him. She knew that what she had to do required every ounce of courage she possessed. She could not continue this way, pretending to be something she was not, nor could she part from him in a way she frankly regarded as dishonest. He had to know the truth about her, and he had to learn it from herself, whatever the consequences.

She said carefully, "People sometimes appear to be quite different from what they are. That could apply to Doctor Halliday as much as to myself."

Colin's glance sharpened. Patsy hurried on breathlessly.

"I mean that beneath the doctor's blunt manner there

178

could be a very kind heart. You can't judge a person by the face they present to the world. Sometimes, a disguise is necessary."

Lesley guessed what was coming. She laid down her coffee cup and said, "I must go". It was better, she thought, for these two to be alone. "If you want me later, Patsy, ring through to my cabin."

"Please stay! I want to tell Colin something and I'll do it better if you're here, because you know what it is."

Colin looked from one to the other. "Go ahead, Patsy. Tell me."

She opened her mouth and closed it again. Lesley stood by, feeling helpless and ineffective. She wanted to shield the girl from Colin's disappointment, to spare her the kind of scene she herself had faced at a similar moment. But there was nothing she could do. Whether she were here to give moral support or not, the actual outcome was one Patsy would have to face alone.

Patsy knew that. She looked at Colin for a long moment and thought sadly: Whatever happens, I'll go on loving him because I just can't stop. Oh, Colin – my poor, misguided Colin! Why can't you throw your greedy ambition overboard and begin again, as a real and proper person?

The silence lengthened and just as Patsy was groping for words and Lesley was seeking some way in which to break the tension, Colin said quietly: "If you're trying to tell me about your money, Patsy, you needn't trouble. I know."

"What do you know?" she asked tautly.

"That you haven't any. That what you had, you spent. That you won it as a prize and blued the lot. And I don't blame you."

"*Colin!*"

Her voice was an incredulous whisper. Lesley felt herself go rigid with shock. Colin looked at them both and smiled a little ruefully.

"Coming from me, that's quite an admission, isn't it? Because you well know the type of man I am, Lesley, and Patsy has already guessed. She asked me the other night if I would ever marry for money. At that time, the answer was yes, even though I'd just learned the truth about her . . . "

Patsy gasped, "How did you learn?"

"Does it matter? Let's say someone told me, and leave it at that."

"Lady Travitt!" Lesley exclaimed. "That newspaper she wouldn't let me throw away!"

"Did it show my photograph?" Patsy demanded. "I thought none would be about now, except around fish and chips somewhere! Certainly not on board the *Regina*."

"Does it matter how I heard?" Colin said again. "The fact remains that I *did* – and my reaction was typical. I took it badly. I decided to have one last wonderful evening with you, then call off the hunt."

"So you *were* after my money," she said sadly.

"Yes. It's useless to pretend. The old lady saw through me, and you saw through me. I hated Lady Travitt for it, but you I admired. It was the first time I'd ever met a girl who recognised me for what I was. It commanded my respect, though I dare say I didn't command yours."

"No, Colin – only my pity."

"*Pity!*"

"I felt sorry for anyone with the wrong set of values. They won't get you the things you want; not happiness and contentment, at least. Once a man starts chasing only material things, there's never any end to it."

"You're a wise little soul, aren't you? Where did you learn such wisdom?"

"In a hard school. An orphanage, then a foster-home, and finally a bed-sit in the suburbs, fighting for myself all along the line. That way you learn what matters – kindness, and being kind in return. All the same, winning a lot of money went to my head, so who am I to condemn *your* wrong sense of values?"

"I think I'd better go," said Lesley.

"Not yet." It was Colin who delayed her now. "This isn't a big renunciation scene. I'm not the type for noble gestures, as you well know, Lesley, though I did try to delude myself, as well as you, on that point. I merely want Patsy to know the truth about me, and I'd like you to hear me admit it."

Patsy said quietly, "But I do know it, Colin. That's why I decided to tell you the truth about myself. There's only one other thing I want to know. You said just now that you'd decided to have one last wonderful evening with me, and then call off the hunt. What stopped you?"

"Your accident."

"You mean you felt sorry for me? You could have kept your pity! I want none of it."

"And you got none of it – no more than the normal pity one feels for an injured person. That wasn't the reason why I was frantic with anxiety over you, nor why I came to see you at every available moment. I could have sent some flowers and a letter of sympathy, and kept discreetly away. Haven't you thought of that?"

"I'm thinking of it now," she managed to whisper.

"What he is trying to tell you," said Lesley, "is that your accident frightened him so badly that he came to his senses. He realised then how much you meant to him. Isn't that it, Colin?"

He looked at her gratefully, and nodded. "That, and more besides. I realised that I'd met a girl who actually meant more to me than money. When I saw you lying at the foot of those steps I – I thought you'd been killed. I was as terrified as a kid. It needed a fright like that to bring things into focus for me – and you with them. Myself, too. And I didn't like the look of myself very much."

This time Lesley really did leave them, and neither heard her go. At the door, she looked back. Colin was kneeling beside the couch, his face buried in Patsy's shoulder, and on the girl's face was an expression of such wonder that it seemed as if the heavens had opened. Never had life been so generous as this. It had given her not riches, but the man she loved. Suddenly Lesley knew that it had done more than that – it had given Patsy a man who, because of her love, would eventually become the man she knew him capable of being.

Lesley walked briskly to the adjoining stateroom and knocked on the door.

Elvira's dry voice cried, "Come in!"

Lesley was momentarily disconcerted to find that the old lady was not alone. Mike was there, sitting in an armchair and smoking his pipe.

"Well, child, and what do you want?"

"Just to know something, Lady Travitt. Why did you show Colin that newspaper, the one with something in it about Patsy Davis? You did, didn't you?"

"Most certainly I did."

Mike took his pipe out of his mouth and demanded, "Why didn't you tell me?"

"Because I didn't want to. I was waiting to see what happened."

"When did you do this?"

"Just before her accident – and you can't accuse me of arranging *that*. Anyway, why should either of you mind?"

"I don't!" Lesley cried. "I came to thank you. He's with her now. She tried to break the news to him, but he forestalled her. He knew all the time and it didn't make any difference! Isn't that wonderful? Want to place any bets on how soon they'll be married?"

She stood there, smiling at them, and the happiness in her smile was very real.

Mike demanded, "You don't mind? But I thought you were in love with the man!"

"So I was – once upon a time."

She blew a kiss to the old lady, and departed.

In two strides, Mike was at the door.

"Wait!" cried Elvira. "You were helping me with this cable to my daughter. What shall I tell her? That you'll meet her when we dock?"

"Tell her this—" cried Mike, and seized the pencil and paper and scribbled furiously. Then he dropped a hurried kiss on her wrinkled cheek, and was gone.

Lady Travitt picked up the paper, and read. For a long moment she stared at it, a slow and satisfied smile spreading across her face, then she leaned back on her pillows and regarded her daughter's photograph almost sadly.

"Carol, my dear, for the first time in your life you're going to be a disappointed young woman. And, my poor darling, I am glad. Perhaps it will make a true woman of you, after all."

Mike saw Lesley's trim figure disappearing down the corridor, and raced after her. Grabbing her unceremoniously by the arm, he commanded, "Come up on deck – I want to talk to you."

"But I—"

"No arguments! This way."

The boat deck was shadowy and deserted. They stood beside the rail, looking out to sea.

"Now," he said. "There are questions I want to ask."

183

Lesley faced him furiously.

"And there are questions *I* want to ask! And, for a change, *I'll* be the one to ask them."

He was so astonished, he could only stare.

"First," she said calmly, "what about Carol?"

"Well, what about her?"

"You were engaged to her, weren't you?"

"I was."

"And it was broken? By whom?"

"By both of us. She preferred a stage life to that of a country G.P.'s wife, and I didn't relish being the husband of a star."

"So you've mistrusted women ever since?"

"If I have, I've been a fool to measure others by her yardstick."

"And now?"

"Perhaps Colin Butler isn't the only man to come to his senses."

"Do you – still love her?"

Lesley's hands clenched the rail tightly. Mike glanced down at them, then at her taut young profile.

"Well," he answered teasingly, "I've just been writing a cable to her. She's coming aboard at New York."

"How nice."

"I hope it will be. It depends, of course."

"On what?"

"On the chances of my cable being correct."

"I don't understand."

"I hope to make you."

"There are other things I don't understand."

"Such as?"

"Why you sacked me; why you hit out the way you did; why you won't take me back; why you say you'll never have me as your ship's nurse again . . . "

"I sacked you in anger – you ought to know by now

that I have a helluva temper. I hit out in a fit of blind jealousy – you ought to know by now that I'm a passionate man. And I won't take you back as my ship's nurse because I don't want you in that capacity. Any other questions?"

"Lots." Her voice shook. "And I can't even think of them right now ... "

"They'll keep," he said gently. "So will mine – except one. And it's all tied up with refusing to have you back as ship's nurse."

"What do you mean?"

"Simply this. When the voyage ends I'm leaving the Owen Line. I'm giving up the sea. I'm going back home to become the country G.P. I always wanted to be. My brother has been holding the fort for me down at Meadowlea – that's the village in Sussex where I was born, and where my father practised for years. I was taking over the practice when he died. Then things went wrong – things which seemed important at the time, but which now don't matter a damn. So my brother took over until I was ready to return. Now he's had a good appointment offered to him in London, and I'm glad of it. So you understand, don't you, why I don't want you to remain as ship's nurse on the *Regina*?"

Lesley's heart was behaving in a ridiculous and uncontrollable fashion.

"Not quite," she answered breathlessly.

"Good heavens, girl, do you want it spelled out for you?"

"Of course I do! All cut and dried, word by word, and delivered in the proper manner."

His arms went about her and he laughed against her hair.

"Very well then – help me to make sure my cable to Carol is correct."

Indignantly, she tried to push him away, but he only laughed the more and held her closer.

"Why should *I* care about your cable?" she cried.

"But think what a fool I'll look if I can't confirm it when she arrives."

Within his grasp, she looked up at him suspiciously.

"Why? What did it say?"

"Simply that I want to introduce her to the girl I'm going to marry. You."

She struggled free.

"Of all the infuriating men, you are the worst I've ever met! No one but you would insult a girl for days on end and then order her to marry you! Excuse me – I must go. I have promised Sister Collard to help her make a dress."

His tall figure blocked her path.

"To hell with Sister Collard's dress! We'll take her to Saks on Fifth Avenue and buy her one to wear at our wedding!"

"Let me *go*!"

But his arms were about her again, and this time there was no breaking free.

"Never!" he whispered. "I'll never let you go, my darling; not now, or ever. So just you try to escape . . . "

Also available this month
TEN titles in the
Mills & Boon ROMANCE Series

FLY BEYOND THE SUNSET *by Anne Hampson*
Faun was a perfectly competent airline pilot — so why, when
she crash-landed in the Borneo jungle, did Clive Tarrant
have to be on board to make things worse?

FLAMINGO MOON *by Margaret Pargeter*
When Eve arrived at Raoul DuBare's house in the Camargue,
he threw her out literally. But Eve came back . . . .

THE LION OF QUIMERA *by Amanda Doyle*
Teresa thought she had applied for a governess's job in Spain,
so how had she ended up on Quimera, off the South
American coast, and tyrannised over by an imposing Marques?

PINEAPPLE GIRL *by Betty Neels*
A grateful patient gave Eloise a pineapple, which she promptly
dropped at Timon van Zeilst's feet — and lost her heart at
the same time!

PORTRAIT OF JAIME *by Margaret Way*
Jaime's grandfather, whom she have never seen, had sent for
her. But if she went, she would be in Quinn Sterling's
power . . . .

A TRIAL MARRIAGE *by Anne Mather*
Rachel was eighteen and Jake twenty years older — rich,
sophisticated, cynical. Could they ever by happy together?

THE WRONG MAN TO LOVE *by Roberta Leigh*
Samantha's inheritance brought her nothing but disaster, for
because of it she met Zachary Farrell — and he had no time
for her at all!

TEMPLE OF THE MOON *by Sara Craven*
A trip to Yucatan should have solved all Gabrielle's problems,
but instead she encountered a new one; the disturbing
Shaun Lennox . . . .

ACROSS A CROWDED ROOM *by Lilian Peake*
Only one man — Rosco Hamden — could save Lisette from
disaster. But could she pay his price?

FRASER'S BRIDE *by Elizabeth Graham*
Everyone said Lara would make the perfect wife for Jerry.
But she fell in love with his brother Matt, who didn't want
her!

Mills & Boon Romances

— all that's pleasureable in Romantic Reading!

Available November 1977 — Only 40p each

THE KING'S SHADOW
Judith Polley

The turbulent days of the Civil War . . . . Katherine Ashley's path is crossed constantly by the King's Shadow and she is caught up in a web of intrigue, blackmail and suspense.

THE FORTUNE-HUNTER
Julia Herbert

Poole Harbour in Georgian times was the smuggling centre of the south coast of England. Against this sinister background, the popular author of THE RUNAWAYS has set a fast-moving, exciting romance.

PURITAN WIFE
Elizabeth de Guise

Constance, a young Puritan orphan, finds her beautiful ancestral home suddenly bestowed on the Royalist Earl of Brede by his grateful sovereign Charles II. Left homeless so dramatically, her only solution is to marry the magnificent Earl, but love him — how can she?

FRANCESCA
Valentina Luellen

Italy in the sixteenth century when the notorious Borgias ruled. Francesca, compelled to marry into the family in order to save her brother's life, finds herself surrounded by treachery and her own life in danger.

Four more exciting titles in our
Masquerade Series
Available October 1977
50p each